D0673673

'What's a beautiful woman like you doing all alone, I wonder?'

The banality of Hazard's words enflamed her. Surely she was worthy of something a little better than that? And then, appallingly, her pain-bruised mind registered the word *alone*, and she could feel the lump gather treacherously in her throat. Oh, God, she couldn't cry now! Not in front of this man.

To punish herself, as much as to get rid of him, Susannah said bitterly, 'If I'm on my own, it's by my own choice, and if you would please...'

'Are you sure that's the truth? Wouldn't it be more honest of you to admit that you're on your own because your lover is with his wife?'

Books you will enjoy
by PENNY JORDAN

SUBSTITUTE LOVER

Gray Chalmers had been a friend to Stephanie when her husband—his cousin Paul—had died in a boating accident. She had never told Gray the truth about her marriage, and had avoided the little town where he and Paul had run a boat-yard together. But now Gray needed her help, and she owed him so much. Could she face the memories?

LEVELLING THE SCORE

Jenna had once loved Simon Townsend—a mere teenage crush, but he had never let her forget it. So when she had a chance of having revenge, she took it. But she didn't bargain for Simon's method of retaliation . . .

FIGHT FOR LOVE

When Natasha had made friends with an old Texan man in London, she had never dreamed that one day he would die and leave her a legacy in his will. It wasn't until she was at his ranch in Dallas that she began to guess at his motives . . .

PAYMENT IN LOVE

It was six years since Heather had seen Kyle Bennett—six years since her childish jealousy had driven him away from the only home he had ever known. But now her father needed his help—and Heather was the only one who could ask for it . . .

SPECIAL TREATMENT

BY

PENNY JORDAN

MILLS & BOON LIMITED
ETON HOUSE   18-24 PARADISE ROAD
RICHMOND   SURREY   TW9 1SR

All the characters in this book have no existence outside the imagination of the Author, and have no relation whatsoever to anyone bearing the same name or names. They are not even distantly inspired by any individual known or unknown to the Author, and all the incidents are pure invention.

All rights reserved. The text of this publication or any part thereof may not be reproduced or transmitted in any form or by any means, electronic or mechanical, including photocopying, recording, storage in an information retrieval system, or otherwise, without the written permission of the publisher.

This book is sold subject to the condition that it shall not, by way of trade or otherwise, be lent, resold, hired out or otherwise circulated without the prior consent of the publisher in any form of binding or cover other than that in which it is published and without a similar condition including this condition being imposed on the subsequent purchaser.

First published in Great Britain 1988 by Mills & Boon Limited

© Penny Jordan 1988

Australian copyright 1988 Philippine copyright 1988 This edition 1988

ISBN 0 263 75975 X

Set in Times Roman 10½ on 12¼ pt. 01-0588-49417 C

Printed and bound in Great Britain by Collins, Glasgow

CHAPTER ONE

THE briefing was over. Rather unsteadily, Susannah got up and hurried out into the corridor, needing the sanctuary of the small cubby-hole that passed for her office.

Her teeth were clenched so hard that her jaw ached, and so did her head. Her nervous system, always the first thing to react when anything upset her, had gone into overdrive.

'You rather got the cold shoulder from our new lord and master, didn't you, darling? I wonder why,' a slow female drawl came from behind her.

Oh, God, the last thing she wanted right now was to have to parry Claire Hunter's acid curiosity!

The older woman had been with the magazine ever since its inception. Where her work was concerned, she was brilliant, quite without equal, witty and clever with her malicious tongue-in-cheek reporting of the foibles and fickleness of the fashionable world, which was her *métier*; but woe betide anyone who forgot to give Claire the recognition she considered her due.

Hazard Maine had not done so, and now *she*, Susannah, was having to pay the price, she reflected wryly, parrying her colleague's inquisitive comment with a dismissive shrug of her shoulders and a casual, 'No idea. New-broom syndrome, I suppose. I just happened to be first in the firing line. That will teach me to arrive at the last minute and get lumbered with a seat in the front row.'

Claire seemed satisfied with her response, and Susannah shut the door of her office behind her in relief. Damn Hazard Maine. Hazard Maine! What sort of a name was that, for God's sake? He was probably American, of course, and his name was almost as familiar to her as her own. Most of his career years had been spent in New York and Sydney, and he had only recently been recalled to head the prestigious *Tomorrow* magazine, which was the flagship of MacFarlane Publishing.

She knew already that they weren't going to get on. But then she had known that ever since Saturday . . .

Susannah closed her eyes momentarily. As if she didn't have enough problems in her life, without adding any more! The very last thing she needed was to be on bad terms with her new boss. She and Richard had got on so well. Richard had encouraged and helped her. Richard . . .

It was pointless wishing Richard back in the editor's seat. His wife, Tom MacFarlane's only child, had made it plain that she was tired of sharing her husband with the demands of a highly successful monthly magazine, and Richard had reluctantly accepted that, unless he wanted to lose his wife, he was going to have to join his father-in-law on the board.

Maybe Aunt Emily was right, and it was Susannah's vibrant chestnut hair that attracted all the problems that seemed to clutter her life. She ought to adopt Claire Hunter's cool, dismissive approach to life, instead of allowing herself to become so involved in the problems of others—problems which inevitably, in some alchemic way, became her own.

Take last Saturday, for instance. Susannah groaned, pushing long, slim fingers into her already unruly curls. God, the very last thing she wanted to do was to remember that!

It had all been David's fault, damn him. Susannah scowled ferociously, glowering at her typewriter.

She had been a fool ever to allow herself to become involved with David Martin, and it didn't help knowing that she had fallen into the same trap as a good proportion of the rest of her sex.

Falling in love with a married man was so... so *tacky*, she fumed, hazel eyes glowing green as her temper got the better of her. She ought to have known... but how could she have done? They had met initially as guests on a local radio chat show. He had been working in television then, she for a local newspaper. They had had so much in common that, when he suggested dinner and a drink after the show, she had not even thought about refusing. Caution had never been one of her strong points and, by the time she had discovered he was married, she was almost in too deep.

It had been a friend who told her, a very concerned and apprehensive girl-friend who had known her for years, and who had guessed that she couldn't know what, apparently, everyone else did—namely, that David was married.

Susannah had taxed him with it, and rather shame-facedly he had admitted that he had deceived her, pleading that it had only been by omission.

At first, he'd pleaded, he had not thought it important to tell her that he was married, and then by the time that it was... Well, he had been too scared of losing her to admit the truth.

Torn between the strength of her feelings—her own impulsiveness and the old-fashioned moral strictures she had grown up with—she hadn't known whether to thank or curse Aunt Emily. Orphaned in the first months of her life, when a freak storm had overturned her father's small boat, killing both her parents, she had been brought up by her only living relative. Being brought up by an elderly spinster, who was more properly her dead father's aunt and not her own, did not equip one for life in the eighties, she had reflected miserably at the time. Another girl would have pushed aside her moral scruples and taken what life offered, but Susannah wasn't like that. David was committed to someone else, and so, heartbreaking though it had been at the time, she had announced to Aunt Emily that it was time she spread her wings, and had started looking for a new job in London.

She had been lucky, thus confirming the old adage about those unlucky in love, or so she had told herself at the time.

In eight months, she had come a long way from the miserable twenty-three-year-old who had left Leicestershire feeling that nothing in life was worth while.

Richard, her boss, had practically adopted her. He had a keen eye for up-and-coming young reporters, whom he took a pride in nurturing and encouraging. She was lucky to have found a job working under him, so she had learned on the newspaper grapevine, and she was forced to concede that it was right. She was just beginning to get back her self-confidence, just beginning to feel that life, after all, might be worth living, albeit a different sort of life from the one she had envisaged that she and David would share, when David himself had shown up in London.

How he had inveigled her address out of Aunt Emily, Susannah didn't know. He had arrived late one cool summer night, when it hadn't stopped raining all day. She had been feeling tired, but exultant. A piece she had done, from an interview with a girl who had accidentally got caught up in a siege situation, had been highly praised by Richard and, as if to confirm that she was at last finding her feet in the fast-paced world of the city, two of Susannah's female colleagues had insisted on her joining them for lunch. They were older than she was, and far more experienced and sophisticated, and it had been a heady experience to have them including her in their conversation as an equal.

She was, they had informed her, marked out as a woman who would go far.

'We owe it to our sex to help and encourage one another. It's time we found a way of beating the Old School Tie male system.'

Susannah had come away from the lunch feeling both elated and drained at the same time, her mind made up. From now on, she was going to concentrate on her career. From now on, no more men for her, married or unmarried.

To open her front door and find David standing there, and, what was worse, to feel her heart lurch in the old familiar way, had been dauntingly depressing.

He had insisted on coming in. He had left Louise, he had told her. Their marriage was over, and he was now free to start a new life with her.

She had been tempted. It was no good pretending that she hadn't. David had wanted to spend the night with her, and she had almost given way. Only the uncomfortable memory of how Aunt Emily would look at her if she knew what Susannah was doing had stopped her. It was ridiculous in this day and age to have such Victorian scruples, but she couldn't help it. Aunt Emily had done her work too well. As a teenager, Susannah had believed that, once she met the man she loved, all her moral doubts about the rights and wrongs of premarital sex would simply fade away, but it wasn't as easy as that.

'What are you trying to tell me?' David had demanded incredulously. 'That we can't make love until we're married?'

Put like that, it sounded archaic, and worse, scheming—as though she was bartering her body for a wedding ring.

'No... It's just that I'm not ready yet, David... I can't explain...'

She had been perilously close to tears, shaking her head to try and blink them away, but to her relief David hadn't been annoyed. Instead he had laughed and taken her into his arms.

'What a fraud you are,' he had teased her. 'What would the world think if they knew that Ms Susannah

Hargreaves, that champion of free will and women's rights, is really a timid little virgin?'

She had been too relieved then to feel angry at his aura of sexual superiority; that had come later. She shivered a little, remembering the glitter of anticipation in his eyes. How much had David wanted her because he genuinely loved her, and how much because he saw her as a challenge?

What did it matter now? There could be nothing between them any more. She had made that abundantly clear to him.

Her flat wasn't large enough for David to stay. It only had one small bedroom, so he had returned to Leicester, telling her that he would be back at the weekend and that they would sit down and make plans for their future together.

Only, before he came back, she had had another visit. This time, from David's wife. Susannah knew her by sight, a small blonde woman, who looked permanently harassed.

The sight of her body, bloated by a very obviously advanced pregnancy, had shocked Susannah even more than her visit. Wordlessly, she had allowed her to walk into the flat, to sit down and to tell her in a savagely bitter monotone that David was demanding a divorce and leaving her with their unborn child. At first, Susannah hadn't been able to take it all in. David's *wife* pregnant...carrying his child? She wasn't completely naïve; she knew that men—for a wide variety of reasons—made love to women for whom they felt little or no emotion. But this child must have been conceived before she had left for London, and now David wanted to pretend that it had never happened.

He wanted to turn his back on his wife and child and simply walk away from them. In that moment, Susannah knew that no matter what she felt for him, she couldn't marry him.

Looking into Louise's white, bloated face, she wasn't sure which of them she pitied and despised the most: Louise, for wanting her husband so desperately that she was prepared to beg like this for him, David, for being so weak that he had allowed his wife to become pregnant and then discarded her, or herself, for not realising the weakness that lay behind that charming smile of his. Well, she realised it now. Aunt Emily had once said to her, when Susannah asked her why she had never married, that she had never found a man she considered worthy of her respect and her trust. Susannah had laughed then, as teenagers do, not understanding what her aunt was telling her, but she understood it now. She loved David, and wanted him, but she did not respect him; she could never lean on him, never trust him.

The interview that followed was burned into her heart for all time. David had pleaded with her, wept tears of frustration and regret, but somehow she managed not to weaken. She had no idea whether or not he intended to go back to his wife. Somehow, she felt that he would, and she sincerely pitied the other woman for all that her life with him would probably be.

She told herself that she had had a narrow escape, that she was the fortunate one, that hers had been the choice, but somewhere deep inside her she still ached and wept for the love she had lost.

And it had been in that mood of bitter self-contempt and misery that she had gone to the Sunderlands' 'do' on Saturday evening.

The Sunderlands were the closest thing she had to godparents. Neil Sunderland had been at school with her father. She had spent many holidays with the family, both at home and abroad, and now that their own two sons were married and living away from home, one in Canada, the other in Australia, she made a point of visiting Neil and Mamie just as often as she could.

Neil had retired earlier in the year from the merchant bank of which he was a director, and they had given up their London house and moved to a small village on the outskirts of Gloucester. Susannah had visited them there several times during the summer and, even though it was the last thing she felt like doing, she knew she would have to go to Mamie's sixtieth birthday party.

Paul and Simon and their respective wives and children were all coming over for the occasion. Susannah was expected to stay the weekend; the house was a large one, with an extensive garden, and Susannah already knew all about the lavish plans for Mamie's party.

Mamie was half-American, which accounted not just for her name, but very probably for her love of life as well. She and Aunt Emily did not get on, and no wonder, Susannah reflected wryly—they were as different as chalk and cheese. She could not imagine any girl brought up by Mamie worrying about the ethics of going to bed with a man to whom she was not married!

She got up clumsily, cursing the lack of space in her office; uncomfortably aware of the fact that using Aunt Emily for an excuse for her lack of sexuality was taking an easy way out. She could feel the starkness of a mood of deep introspection crowding in on her, like a winter's afternoon obliterating the light. How she resented this side of her nature, this dark, and sometimes frightening, gloom that came down over her without warning, engulfing and possessing her.

No doubt, like her temper, it went with her hair, and so perhaps it did, part of a Celtic heritage, like her pale delicate skin and stormy green eyes.

And it hadn't helped having Hazard Maine ripping into her like that. It was the worst of bad luck that he should have spotted that yawn she had tried to smother behind her hand.

Of course, she hadn't found what he was saying boring—quite the contrary. How could anyone be bored when listening to a diatribe against the skills of an editorial staff among which one numbered? It hadn't just been to cover up that she had accused him of wanting to behave like a traditional new broom. She had been so happy working for Richard. Susannah scowled, wondering for how long she would be given the opportunity to continue working for the magazine. Hazard Maine didn't like her. To judge from his lecture to them this morning, he didn't like any of them. He had attacked the magazine, throwing them all off guard, warning them that he intended to make changes. But surely those cold grey eyes had rested on her face just momentarily longer than they had on anyone else's?

To her horror, she had had to stifle another yawn. This time, he hadn't even attempted to soften his contempt.

'Work comes first for anyone who wants to succeed on this magazine, Ms Hargreaves,' he had told her crisply. 'That being the case, I suggest you either change your job—or your lover.'

She had flushed scarlet, mortified by the ripple of amusement that ran through the room, and all too aware of the speculative glances of her male colleagues. She had a reputation for being cool and unapproachable. Her private life was something she never discussed at work, and with one short sentence Hazard Maine had created an image of her life-style that was totally false, and yet which she was completely unable to correct.

She knew *why* he had picked on her, of course. Her full mouth tightened angrily. He might be a big man in size, well over six foot and athletically muscled, but he certainly wasn't in spirit. To hold what had happened on Saturday against her like that ... Of all the bad luck! She had never imagined—but then why should she? Neil and Mamie moved in completely different circles from those she inhabited. She had never dreamed ...

But then, the weekend had gone disastrously wrong, right from the start ...

She sat back in her chair, trembling.

CHAPTER TWO

SHUTTING the door of her flat behind her with her shoulder, Susannah put down the box she was carrying. Her arms ached and she flexed them gratefully. A quick cup of coffee, change into her travelling clothes and then she could be away.

Trust Mamie not to warn her until the last minute that it was going to be a formal 'do'. White tie and tails, no less! She had been lucky to be able to find a dress to fit her at such short notice. She was only a size eight, and the dress hire shop she had rung up in a state of panic had told her that they stocked very few extra-small sizes.

The dress she had chosen was quite plain. She wasn't in the mood for dressing up in anything eye-catching. She wasn't in the mood for anything other than her own company, if the truth were known, but if she failed to turn up Mamie would pick and question until she had got at the truth, and the last thing she wanted was for worldly, sophisticated Mamie to know what a fool she had made of herself.

They had an odd relationship—sometimes friends, sometimes enemies—and there were times when Susannah envied Mamie's daughters-in-law the oceans that separated them from her inquisitive tongue. And yet she knew Mamie loved her.

'Don't be frightened of life,' she was always urging her. 'Jump in and enjoy it.'

16

'Susannah isn't the jumping-in type. We British aren't,' Neil had palliated, and yet somehow even his kind words left a slight sting.

A sting that was intensified now. How much of her rejection of David had to do with what she genuinely believed to be right, and how much was because she was terrified of the implications of committing herself to him? Was it because Emily had always held her firmly at a distance that she herself was unable to allow anyone to get close, really close to her?

Angry with herself, she hurried into her bedroom, pulling a brush through her tangled curls, and quickly changing out of her jeans and sweatshirt into the separates she had bought for herself the previous week.

At first sight, pink and black might not seem the best choice of colours for a redhead, but she had the colouring to get away with them, and the pink was of that soft, intensely feminine variety that made those who could not wear it gnash their teeth with envy.

The dress, her case and the present she had bought for Mamie were all speedily packed into her Fiesta, the flat locked up and the alarm set. She should be there in time for lunch. The afternoon would probably be taken up with a multitude of last-minute tasks for Mamie, and then there would only be the evening to be got through. Thank God, Mamie knew nothing about David...David... Even now, part of her wished...

What? she derided herself. That by some magic process he could miraculously be free? But he *wasn't* free, and she didn't think she could live with herself or him, knowing that he was prepared to turn his back on his child. Susannah wasn't sentimental where children were concerned, but she had been brought up to recognise the importance of facing up to one's responsibilities. And, if she was honest with herself, she didn't know how she would cope with loving a man who had already previously committed himself to another woman.

Stop thinking about him, she admonished herself. It's over...

Easier said than done, but one look at her face would alert Mamie to the fact that something was wrong, and then she would pry and question, and Susannah really didn't think she was capable of dealing with Mamie's curiosity, however well meant.

She tried to think about something else—about the praise Richard had given her for that piece on the siege victim. He had been enthusiastic and flattering about her talent. He had prophesied that she would go far. But Richard was leaving and Hazard Maine was taking his place. What would he be like, this American who had spent his life between continents, when he wasn't reporting from some war-torn part of the globe?

She had read up his biog. They all had, once they had known that he was taking over the editor's chair. He was thirty-four years old, ten years older than she was; unmarried. That had surprised her until she remembered that he had been a war correspondent, and war correspondents rarely married. He had edited papers in New York and Sydney, and now he was going to head *Tomorrow*, MacFarlane's most prestigious publication.

Jokes had flown round the office about 'wild colonial hicks' and 'clever New York hacks', but none of them really knew what they were going to have to face. He had a formidable reputation; he was coming in with the power to hire and fire at will, to make his own rules and to do what he wished with the magazine. They had heard that much on the grapevine. Just as they had also heard that, at first, he had turned down the job, claiming that he was a newspaper man and that magazines, no matter how highly prized, did not interest him.

At least, that was the gist of what he had said. Rumour had it that his actual phraseology had been considerably more earthy!

Apart from being rather in awe of his professional reputation, Susannah had no strong feelings about Hazard Maine. She had run out of feelings of any kind. She simply felt she wanted to be left alone to pick up the pieces of her life. She knew that she was going to miss Richard. One or two of the staff had teased her about him, but no one who knew Richard could ever seriously imagine that his interest in her was anything other than professional.

Richard was very much in love with his wife. He had to be to give up a job he loved to take one in which he had very little interest but, as he had told Susannah, he felt he owed it to Caroline.

'Newspaper men don't make good husbands, she says, and she's quite right. Now that the boys are growing up, they need me around. At the moment, I only really see them at weekends, and then not always as much as I should.'

Like her, Richard had been brought up with what was now considered an old-fashioned code of ethics.

Susannah liked and admired him. She knew she was going to miss him, as a boss and as a mentor.

Neil and Mamie's 'new' home was a seventeenth-century manor house, approached by a narrow curling drive that hid the stone façade with its mullioned windows from view right until the last moment.

Mamie, with typical American energy and enterprise, had had the inside almost completely gutted since moving in. Experienced and expensive designers had been brought in, and Susannah, who had rather liked the original shabby comfort of the place, was not particularly looking forward to seeing the changes they had wrought.

Several cars were already parked in front of the house, and she reversed her Fiesta into a small space left to one side of a large and very new-looking Jaguar saloon. She always parked next to new cars if she could. It meant the owners were likely to be that bit more careful about opening their doors on her paintwork, or so she always hoped.

The front door opened as she walked towards it and Mamie hurried out to embrace her. The soft tweed skirt, the pastel cashmere sweater, the pearls, all of them were perfectly co-ordinated, and so obviously chosen to fit in with their wearer's background, that Susannah had to suppress a faint grin. Typical Mamie!

'You're too thin,' she was told firmly. 'And too pale. What have you been doing with yourself?'

'Working,' Susannah told her. 'And, as for being too thin, I thought no woman could be that.'

'There's thin, and then there's *thin*,' Mamie pronounced darkly. 'And you, my girl, are *thin*. It doesn't suit you.'

'Thanks, Mamie.'

Elegant eyebrows lifted towards the older woman's beautifully styled silver-grey hair. 'My goodness, you are prickly today.' The smooth, unlined forehead creased slightly. 'Susannah, is something wrong?'

Oh, heavens, this was the last thing she needed! Susannah bit down hard on her bottom lip. 'No, I ... You're right. I think I must have been working too hard. If I apologise for feeling grouchy, will you show me round the house?'

She linked her arm through Mamie's, deliberately forcing herself to withstand the older woman's concerned inspection.

'Apology accepted,' Mamie said at last, patting her hand. 'And don't worry. I won't indulge myself by taking you up on your self-sacrificing offer.' She made a small *moue*. 'I know that you preferred the house as it was before. You're just like Neil. He thought we would move in and not touch a thing,' she scoffed. 'You English. How you hate change!'

They laughed together, harmony restored, and Susannah allowed herself to feel a small surge of relief. She had forgotten how sharp Mamie could be. She would have to be careful not to betray herself again. She knew that both Mamie and Neil were deeply fond of her. She had no wish to spoil their party by giving them cause for concern.

'Have Paul and Simon arrived yet?'

'Last night.' Mamie rolled her eyes heavenwards. 'Much as I love my grandchildren, I have to admit that *en masse* ...'

'What's that, Ma? Not tired of us already?'

Paul was the image of Neil, his father, Susannah reflected, as the younger of the two boys enveloped her in a bear hug.

'And how's our little red-headed godsister? Good heavens, girl, what have you been doing to yourself? There's nothing of you!'

'That's just what I've been telling her.'

'Where are Sarah and the boys?' Susannah asked, disentangling herself from Paul's hug.

'We're all in the conservatory. Come on in. Ethel's just made coffee.'

Ethel was the housekeeper who had been with Mamie and Neil for as long as Susannah had known them. At first, she had flatly refused to leave London, but somehow Mamie had persuaded her.

As they walked into the conservatory, Susannah could see out into the large rear garden, where a marquee had been erected. The whole area was a busy hive of activity, with caterers dashing to and fro, and florists still putting the final touches to their work.

Susannah already knew the two girls Simon and Paul had married, although two new babies had been added to the family since she had last seen them, and they had to be duly admired and cuddled before she could turn her attention to their grandfather.

Retirement suited Neil, she admitted, smiling at him. He was a gentler character than Mamie. Not perhaps as shrewd, but very astute in his own way.

Lunch was a relaxed affair, the conversation flowing freely. It had been almost twelve months since the whole family had last been together, and there was a good deal of gossip to catch up on. Susannah was quite content to sit on the sidelines, putting in the odd comment where appropriate.

'And what about you, Susannah?' Simon asked. 'Still with the magazine?'

'Yes...and still loving it.'

Was that a touch of defiance in her voice? Much as she liked both men, there was no getting away from the fact that Paul and Simon were rather old-fashioned when it came to women and careers. Both their wives seemed more than content with their family and home lives, but Sarah had been a consultant before marriage, and Emma a highly successful model.

Neither of them, it seemed, missed their busy careers. Was that what love did for you? Susannah wondered bleakly. Did it rob you of all ambition and drive? Had she felt like that about David? Would she have been content to change her whole life-style and to stay at home while he...

While he betrayed her as he had done his wife?

The unpalatable thought wouldn't go away. This, she knew, was what lay at the root of her determination to break away from him—this fear, this lack of trust.

'Hey, where have you gone?'

Teasingly, Simon tugged her hair, bringing her out of her thoughts and back into the conversation.

This was the closest thing she had ever known to real family life, and yet even here she remained on the fringe...outside the magic, charmed circle, in some way.

Gradually, the lunch party broke up. Mamie had to talk to the caterers, Neil had some phone calls to make. The children were getting fractious and were borne away by their respective mothers. Paul and Simon were deep in some private conversation. Susannah got up and started to collect the empty plates. She might as well see if she could give Ethel a hand in the kitchen.

Susannah was upstairs in her room, getting ready, when she heard the first of the guests arrive. Late in the afternoon she had gone for a walk, and had been away longer than she had planned. Walking eased her thoughts, it also brought back painful memories. Why was it possible to miss a man she knew she was better off without? She did miss David, even though she knew she had made the right decision.

Sighing faintly, she towelled the last of the moisture from her shower off her skin. Her hired dress was still in its box, and belatedly she remembered that she ought to have got it out and pressed it. She shrugged fatalistically. It was too late now and, besides, Mamie was the star of the evening. No one was likely to notice a few creases in her rather drab dress.

She opened the box, frowning slightly as she caught the shimmer of blue through the tissue paper. Blue... The dress she had chosen was grey, surely?

Uncertainly she lifted it out of the paper, her mouth falling open in shock. This wasn't the dress she had hired! Dry-mouthed with shock, she stared at it. This was nothing like the dress she had hired. This... Never in a thousand lifetimes would she ever have chosen anything as exotic, as downright...provocative as this dress, with its tightly moulded bodice and its flaring thirties-style fishtail flouncing skirt.

The ruched bodice glittered and sparkled beneath her fingers. She couldn't wear it! But she had no option. Already she was late.

Cursing beneath her breath, she looked at the underwear she had already laid out. There was no way she was going to be able to wear a bra underneath it.

Gritting her teeth, she pulled it on, not daring to look at her reflection for several seconds.

When she did, she was amazed by how red the intense blue made her hair appear, and how white her skin. Aunt Emily would most definitely not approve; the dress was everything *she* deplored. It wasn't so much that it was actually vulgar—indeed, the neckline was relatively modest—but it was the way the ruched fabric hugged every line of her torso right down to her knees before flaring out in that provocative fishtail froth of net and silk.

She couldn't wear it. She was just about to take it off when Mamie walked into her room.

The older woman looked elegant and *soignée* in a dress of soft coral silk. Her eyebrows lifted when she saw Susannah.

'Oh my, that really is something!'

'They gave me the wrong dress,' Susannah told her weakly. 'This is nothing like what I was intending to wear.'

To her shock, Mamie chuckled.

'Oh, my dear, if you could just see your face! It suits you, you know. The whole effect is very... very challenging: provocative and yet coolly remote. It will drive the men wild.'

'I don't *want* to drive them wild,' Susannah told her crossly. 'Mamie, I can't wear this...'

'Unless you've brought something else with you, you're going to have to,' Mamie told her crisply, adding caustically, 'Susannah, for heaven's sake! You aren't your Aunt Emily, you know. There is nothing wrong with the dress, and it suits you to perfection. You're a woman, not a child; just for once in your life *be* one.'

She was gone before Susannah could retaliate. Was that how people saw her? she wondered miserably. Mamie had made her feel like some kind of freak, like ... Oh, for goodness' sake, what was she getting so worked up about? It was only a dress. What did it matter if it *wasn't* the one she had chosen?

Her head lifted, her chin tilting proudly. So Mamie thought she didn't know how to be a woman, did she?

Head held high, she made her way downstairs.

Neil and Mamie weren't having a formal receiving line, so Susannah was free to mingle with the guests who had already arrived: old friends of Mamie and Neil's from London in the main, people she already knew and felt quite at ease with.

It wasn't until she saw Simon that she realised how dramatically different the dress made her look. His eyebrows lifted, his mouth pursed in a silent whistle.

'Wow! What happened to you, Red?' he demanded teasingly.

'Nothing,' she told him flatly, both irritated and at the same time faintly embarrassed by his openly male inspection of her. 'And don't look at me like that.'

'No, don't,' agreed his wife, Emma, joining them and giving Susannah a friendly smile. 'Love your outfit. Lucky you to be able to wear it.' She grimaced ruefully and patted her hips. 'I do envy you being so slim.'

'Nonsense, woman, you're perfect as you are,' Simon told her firmly. 'Are you sure you're up to the consequences of wearing an outfit like that?' he teased Susannah over his shoulder as he took his wife's arm. 'If not ...'

'Stop tormenting her, Simon,' Emma commanded him, firmly leading him away.

But it was too late, the damage was done; Susannah immediately felt awkwardly conspicuous, her small stock of courage dwindling away. The best thing she could do would be to find herself a dark corner and to hide away in it until she could safely escape to her room. Aunt Emily had been right, she thought grimly, men *did* judge a woman on how she dressed. She had never really thought about it before, but now she could see what her aunt meant.

Normally, she didn't waste much time or concern over her clothes; her life was far too busy for that. Comfortable, loose-fitting skirts or well worn jeans comprised her normal working wear. Busy reporters didn't have time to worry about looking glamorous.

Glamorous? She made a face at herself in the rococo mirror hanging in the hall. What an out-of-date word! But then, she *was* out of date, in some respects, at least. She still felt bruised and sore from her last meeting with David. He had accused her then of leading him on, of being a 'tease', although his language had been stronger and very offensive. She had seen him in a new light then—not just as a weak man, but as an unkind one as well. She told herself that she had had a lucky escape, but that didn't make the pain inside go away.

The interior designers had done their work well, she admitted as she slipped into Neil's study in order to avoid the chattering group of people making their way down the hall.

When she had first seen the house, before Neil and Mamie had moved in, this room had been very neglected, the panelling on the walls in a very poor state of repair. Now it had been cleaned and treated, the stone fireplace restored and Neil's antique partner's desk installed, the designer touches showing only in the clever co-ordination of fabrics and ornaments. She rather liked the richness of the paisley fabric chosen for the curtains, she admitted. It went well with the heaviness of the dark red leather chesterfield. This would be a comfortable retreat for Neil, somewhere where he could come to read his papers and escape.

Behind her, the door opened and she stiffened, surprised out of her resentment at being discovered by the unexpectedness of Richard's familiar voice. 'My goodness, you do look...'

'Don't, please,' Susannah begged, interrupting him. 'I think I've already heard as much as I want to hear about my changed appearance from Simon.'

She knew she sounded far more irritated than the circumstances warranted, and it wasn't Richard's fault that the shop had got their orders muddled up. She bit her lip and apologised.

'I'm sorry, Richard...'

'Don't be. And don't apologise. Truthfully, my dear, you look lovely. It's just that I'm more used to seeing you in rather more mundane outfits. I didn't realise you knew the Sunderlands.'

'Neil and Mamie are the closest thing I have to a family. Neil and my father were at school together. I must admit, though, that I didn't realise *you* knew them.'

'I don't—not really. Caroline and Mamie have become great friends though, both of them being newcomers into the area, so to speak. I came in here to escape the hustle for a while. Parties aren't really my cup of tea.'

But he would never deny Caroline the pleasure of attending them, Susannah thought enviously. He was too kind, too considerate to spoil his wife's pleasure. If only David could have been more like Richard... She sighed faintly, and instantly Richard frowned in concern.

'Is something wrong? I must admit I've been worrying about you lately. It isn't this change of editor business that's worrying you, is it? There's no need, I promise you. I've given Hazard a glowing report on you, and one that you well deserve. He's not an easy man to get along with, I admit, but he's a very fair one.'

'It... it isn't work.'

She could have bitten her tongue out for letting the admission escape, and the instant she looked into Richard's face, she guessed that he had already known.

'Romance troubles, eh?' he asked sympathetically. 'Poor Susannah! Would it help to talk about things?'

Susannah shook her head, appalled by the sudden rush of weak tears flooding her eyes and clogging her throat. What on earth was the matter with her? Aunt Emily had brought her up to keep her emotions strictly under control, and here she was, behaving like . . .

'Come on, now! It can't be as bad as all that.'

The comforting arm Richard put round her shoulders was the last straw. To her utter chagrin, she found herself bursting into tears.

'Come on, now. Whoever he is, he isn't worth getting into this state over. There are always other fish in the sea, Susannah. Besides, you've got a good career ahead of you . . .'

As she listened to Richard's soothing voice, she fought to get herself back under control. He was so kind, so gentle, and she felt the worst kind of fool for crying all over him like this.

'Come on,' he coaxed gruffly, 'it will be all right. You'll see.'

As she lifted her head from his shoulder, Susannah thought she saw someone walk past the open study door. Suddenly conscious of the fact that anyone could walk in and see them, she pulled away from him, mustering a weak smile.

'I'm being a complete idiot, and you're quite right. He isn't worth crying over.'

'That's OK, what else are ex-bosses for?'

'I'd better go upstairs and do something about my face.'

As she turned to leave him, Richard caught hold of her arm and said soberly, 'It's a very good face, you know, Susannah. Even more important, there's a very good brain behind it. Whoever he is, he just isn't worth what you're putting yourself through.'

With another watery smile, she left him and hurried up to her room. Apart from a suspicious pinkness round her eyes, she didn't look too bad, but, as she discovered when she attempted to reapply the small amount of make-up she normally used, it took rather more eyeshadow and mascara than usual to conceal the evidence of her tears. She wasn't quite sure if she liked the very heavy-lashed effect produced by the extra mascara; it gave her an unfamiliar, almost sultry look.

Shrugging aside the thought, she hurried back downstairs. She was here as Neil and Mamie's guest, and she mustn't spoil their party by letting them worry about her.

As luck would have it, Mamie was walking across the hall just as Susannah went back downstairs. 'Are you all right?' she asked suspiciously.

'Fine. I didn't realise you knew Richard, my ex-boss . . .'

'Richard? Oh yes, of course, Caroline's husband. Heavens, what a coincidence! I really had no idea . . .'

Having successfully distracted her, Susannah made her escape, pleading thirst.

In point of fact, there was nothing she felt less like doing than drinking champagne and chatting with people who were, in the main, strangers. She wanted to go home and be alone to nurse her hurts, she acknowledged painfully. But what was the point? David wasn't worth her tears, or her anguish. Savagely, she told herself over and over again, almost as though she was repeating a powerful spell, that she was better off without him, that it was David's wife who was to be pitied. She had been lonely and David had seen that loneliness and played on it, gradually drawing her deeper and deeper into a relationship which he had known all along was wrong.

Once inside the marquee, she headed for a quiet corner, close to one of the ornate floral decorations. Here she could see without being seen, and with luck escape Mamie's alert eyes.

If she admitted the truth, she was still suffering from the after-effects of that appalling interview with Louise, David's wife. The extent to which the other woman had had to degrade herself hurt Susannah; ridiculously, she felt both shame and resentment for Louise on behalf of their shared sex. She didn't love David any more; how could she? She had deluded herself as to his real personality; the man she had thought she loved had been an ideal, an adolescent's dream. The reality was the reason for her anguish and shame, she acknowledged, raw with the newness of her emotions. Her hand shook a little, and in a fit of self-disgust she took a deep swallow of her champagne. It tasted tart and sour, like her whole life, she derided herself bitterly, impulsively tipping what was left in her glass into a convenient plant-pot.

It was only as she turned round that she realised that she had been observed. Not by anyone she knew. The man watching her with such compelling eyes was a complete stranger.

His evening clothes had quite obviously been tailored for him; they fitted far too well to have been bought off the peg.

At some time or another in his life he must have indulged in some sort of punishingly physical sport, she guessed, noting the width of his shoulders and the leanness of his torso. He was tanned, not a summer holiday tan, but the tan of someone who had spent long, long hours in the sun. His hair was black and very thick. It was also a shade too long, she noted disapprovingly, its length rather at odds with the so-phisticated elegance of his evening-dress clothes. Surely a man whose clothes fitted as well as this one's did could afford to have a decent hair-cut? Her forehead creased in a slight frown, her reporter's mind, trained to notice even the smallest anomalies, registered the oddly discordant note of the length of that thick dark hair and queried it. Was it simply that he preferred it that length and didn't give a damn about what the rest of the world thought? Was it . . .

Abruptly, she realised that she was staring at him, and that, worse, he was regarding her with a look of insolent knowingness that made her blood burn in a dark red tide of betrayal over her body.

As clearly as though he had spoken the words across the space that divided them, she sensed his sexual ap-praisal. It was the dress, of course, she realised bit-terly. That was why he was looking at her as though she were some sort of commodity for sale. And yet, behind the arrogant contempt, she had glimpsed, if only for a second, something more dangerous: some-thing male and predatory that made her skin tingle and her body quiver. Sexual chemistry at its most potent. And, ridiculously, she had had the distinct impression that he had been as startled by it as she had herself in those few seconds of mental awareness they had exchanged before he had recovered himself and guarded his expression from her.

It was the dress. It *had* to be the dress. She just did
not have that sort of effect on men, especially not on
men as blatantly masculine as that one. Everything
about him had shrieked that he was a man used to
having his own way. It had all been there, in the nar-
rowed, assessing scrutiny of his eyes, and that hard,
chiselled outline of his profile. He was about Simon's
age, early thirties or thereabouts, and he looked as
though he had lived every one of those years to the
full.

He was no David, she thought ironically.

Annoyed with herself, she clenched her hands. It
didn't matter who he was, she wasn't interested. The
last thing she wanted was to get herself involved with
another man, especially one who thought she was the
sort of woman portrayed by the dress she was wearing.

'What's the matter? Wasn't the champagne an acceptable vintage?'

The derisory sting of his voice shocked her into a
frozen pose of surprise. Where had he come from?
He must have moved so quickly and quietly. Instinctively, she looked across the room to where he had
been and heard him give a soft, satisfied laugh.

'Quite acceptable, thank you,' she told him dismissively, hiding her shock.

Close to, Susannah realised she had been right about
that sun. It had burned tiny lines either side of his
eyes. Pale grey eyes, she noticed, rimmed by a much
darker edge. It took a tremendous effort of will-power
to drag her own gaze away from them.

Her whole body suddenly felt weak and vulnerable.
She started to move away, her voice cool and dismissive. She wasn't some cheap pick-up, whatever

conclusions he had drawn about her from her outfit, and if he didn't take her hint and take himself off right away he would soon discover his mistake.

A tiny shock thrilled through her as she discovered how much she was relishing the pleasure of putting him down. What was happening to her? What sort of woman was she turning into? She had seen at first hand how hard and embittered some of her older female colleagues had become, and she didn't want to end up like that. They were so cynical and worldly; time and humankind had destroyed all their illusions and hardened them so that they were incapable of having any real feelings. She couldn't live like that.

'What's a beautiful woman like you doing all alone, I wonder?'

The banality of his words enflamed her. Surely she was worthy of something a little better than that? And then, appallingly, her pain-bruised mind registered the word *alone*, and she could feel the lump gather treacherously in her throat. Oh, God, she couldn't cry now! Not in front of this man.

To punish herself, as much as to get rid of him, she said bitterly, 'If I'm on my own, it's by my own choice, and if you would please . . .'

'*Your* choice?' She flinched beneath the derision in his voice. 'Are you sure that's the truth? Wouldn't it be more honest of you to admit that you're on your own because your lover is with his wife?'

How on earth had he known? Was her guilt written in her eyes for everyone to see? Susannah wanted to cower back from him and hide her face, but pride kept her standing where she was. She wasn't prepared for this. She would never be prepared for it. She remembered how sick she had been after Louise had gone, and she felt a return of that nausea now.

She made to push past him and he caught hold of her, his voice rasping as he derided acidly, 'Running away? What's wrong? Can't you face up to the truth? Can't you admit that you haven't got the guts to find your own man; that you prefer to steal someone else's?'

Susannah looked round in panic. Couldn't someone see what was happening? She almost expected him to lift her off her feet and to shake her like a terrier with a rat. Her breath was locked in her throat, her heart thumping in rapid, shallow strokes.

'How innocent you look. Like a child cowering in fear of the dark. But you aren't innocent, are you?'

She wanted to deny it, to demand by what right he spoke to her like this. But to her horror she heard herself saying weakly instead, 'How did you know? How...'

And then, frighteningly, the room went dark all around her and started to sway. Noise rode over her in waves, like echoes from a sea shell. She just had time to realise, in horror, that she was actually fainting, before everything went black.

When Susannah came round, she was lying on the chesterfield in Neil's study.

The door was closed. Susannah struggled to sit up, and gasped as she felt the top of her dress fall away. As she clutched it to her in frantic embarrassment, she saw someone move.

Her heart chopped as she watched her antagonist detach himself from the shadows and come towards her.

'Mamie——' she demanded weakly.

'We don't want to spoil her party, do we? Besides, you're all right now. That's quite an art,' he added callously, 'fainting to order. Got you out of more than one tight situation, no doubt.'

How dared he? How dared he imply that she... Oh, it really was too much! She sat up again, forgetting her dress until it was too late, and the fierce burning heat of his gaze grazed over her naked breasts.

She made a small choking sound in her throat, a mixture of embarrassment and fear, her hands instinctively moving protectively to conceal her body.

As his fingers caught her wrists, she winced in shocked pain, but despite all her efforts she was unable to stop him from pushing her hands down.

He was closer to her now. She could feel his breath against her forehead. His fingers were hard, and yet curiously warm against her wrists. His thumb stroked across her racing pulse.

'You should have been an actress. So much manufactured emotion! And why? You can't really expect me to believe I'm the first man to see you like this.'

His derision taunted her. Even she could feel the unsteady racing of her pulse beneath his touch. What was he trying to do to her?

An awful, untenable thought shook her, and as though he had read her mind his face hardened.

'You don't really think I'd degrade myself by committing rape? Oh, come on.' His mouth twisted, his eyes derisive.

'Why did you bring me in here?' She was breathing shallowly, as though her body wanted to conserve what was left of its weak strength. 'My dress...'

'You fainted, and I unzipped the back of your *dress*...so that you could breathe unhindered.'

His unspoken statement on the extreme tightness of her dress infuriated her. She tried to pull herself away from him.

'Yes, well...but I'm all right now and, if you don't mind, I'd like to get dressed.'

'Oh, but I do mind.'

Susannah stared at him.

'Oh, come on! Don't pretend to be surprised. You must be used to the way men react to the sight of your body by now. What do you think is so different about me that would stop me from enjoying the view? Or are you frightened your lover might walk in and discover us?'

Her *lover*?

Confused, she stared at him. She had experienced so many unfamiliar emotions in such a short space of time, she scarcely knew what she thought any more.

'I... He won't,' she told him absently.

The way he was looking at her was having the oddest effect on her senses. It was almost as though he were in some way hypnotising her. His fingers still touched her wrists, but their touch now was a persuasive caress that made her skin tingle and her breath catch. It was all so unfamiliar to her. David had never had time for such light, teasing loveplay.

Loveplay! Horrified, she pulled away, and his hand accidentally brushed against her breast. The quiver of sensation that shot through her at that touch terrified her.

'I must go.'

She said it like a sleep-walker, struggling to sit up, her eyes fixed on the door, and the reality that lay beyond it. Here, in this room, she seemed to have strayed into an unknown dimension. Who was this man? What was she doing with him?

She made to get up, but he caught hold of her, his hands hard against her narrow bare ribcage.

'No,' he denied harshly and, as her heart leapt in terror, he repeated the denial more softly, his head bending towards her. She felt his breath feather against her skin, caught the clean scent of it and then shuddered, caught up in a mindless complexity of emotions as his hands moved to cup her breasts, his weight bearing her backwards into the chesterfield, his fingers fanning out possessively against her paler flesh as his mouth whispered against hers.

'No, I'm not letting you go yet. I rescued you, remember? And now I'm claiming my reward.'

Rescued her? From what? A faint that he himself had induced? Round and round in crazy circles spun her mind, faster and faster, until she was unable to catch hold of anything stable and real. Beneath his mouth her own softened, unable to withstand the skilled precision of its movements. She felt his tongue caressing her too vulnerable flesh; heard herself moan deeply in her throat as her body, denied fulfilment of its femininity in her relationship with David, accepted and welcomed the maleness of him. Her mouth opened, her head bending back beneath the force of his kiss. He made a sound against her lips, masculine and savage in its arousal. His body moved against her own, hard and . . .

Shock coursed through her. What on earth was she doing? She wrenched her mouth from his, but he ignored her attempt to break free, his lips moving unhurriedly along the slope of her shoulder and down towards her breast. She arched her back, frantic to get away from him, and then every muscle in her body stilled as his lips captured the taut pinnacle of her nipple and drew on it so fiercely and sweetly that every single one of her senses became fixated on what she was experiencing.

Such physical pleasure! Why had she never known it had existed? David's hurried fumbling attempts to caress her between quarrels had in no way prepared her for this. She was drowning in delight and loving it.

She must have made some sound, because abruptly he released her, his mouth moving arousingly against her moist skin as he muttered, 'You liked that? Do you want more?'

And before she could speak he was drawing her back into his mouth, sucking on her with a slow and erotic deliberation that made her forget everything but the necessity of ensuring that such pleasure never stopped.

'I want you. You know that, don't you?'

The savage words cut through the intensity of her dazed pleasure. She looked up at him. His lashes were so dark and thick. She wanted to reach out and touch him. His skin was flushed, and slightly damp. She could feel the heat burning along his cheekbones as he pressed his face against her skin. He *did* want her. She exulted in the knowledge.

'Is this how you entrapped him? With the lure of your body and your pseudo-innocence? Oh God, I...'

The savage disgust in his voice hurt. Susannah wanted to tell him that he was wrong, that this was something she had never shared with any other man and never would, and then reality struck her, starkly and inescapably. What was she doing?

She took advantage of his momentary relaxation to push him away.

He released her, and then cursed as she sprang off the chesterfield, tugging her dress on, her eyes glittering with green fire.

'Don't you dare come anywhere near me! Don't touch me.' Her voice shook, but she was back in control of herself now. 'I don't know who you are, or what you think you're doing... I don't know what you think gives you the right to—question me!'

'Don't you?' His voice was flat and derisive. 'Odd, I could have sworn that not so very long ago you knew exactly what it was.'

The way his glance lingered on her breasts made his meaning all too clear. Before she left this room, she had to convince him that he meant nothing to her. Nothing at all. Her pride demanded it. What had happened was too demeaning—so shocking. She moved and winced as her stimulated breasts thrust demandingly against the constraining fabric of her dress, her awareness of her own arousal increasing her humiliation. How could she ever have allowed herself to be caught in such a situation, and with a complete stranger?

'Oh, that,' she told him coolly, striving for detachment and self-control. 'Please don't take it personally. It's been rather a long time since I was last—with my lover.'

She shrugged, triumph buoying her up as she caught the fierce glitter of anger darkening his eyes, knowing that he wanted to reject what she was saying. She was hurting his pride and she was glad, fiercely glad.

'Men don't have the monopoly on sexual frustration, you know,' she told him.

'You . . .' He lunged towards her, but as she backed off he stopped, his face contorting with savage bitterness. 'You wanted me,' he told her flatly.

'No,' she corrected him acidly, 'I wanted a man...any man, if you want me to be totally honest.' Her eyebrows lifted as she viewed his bitter, dark face. 'Oh, come on. You look like a sophisticated man. Surely you didn't think I was overcome with passion for *you*?'

He looked as though he wanted to kill her, thought Susannah, torn between exultation and stark, terrifying fear. What on earth had she done? What on earth was she *going* to do if he refused to believe her? But no, he was turning on his heel and walking towards the door.

At the door, he stopped and turned to look at her.

'With luck, you and I will never meet again,' she told him sweetly.

'Don't be too sure.'

A threat? But why? He couldn't want to see her again. Shrugging slightly, she waited until she was sure he had gone and then hurried up to her room.

One look in her mirror told her that she had made a wise decision. Her lips, bare of lip gloss, still looked swollen from his kiss. Her eyes glittered with febrile arousal, and her breasts—— Guiltily, she stared down at where they strained against her dress, her nipples hard and erect. She touched them, covering them with trembling hands, as though to protect herself from harm.

Weak with shock and reaction, she collapsed on to her bed. What on earth had got into her? Thank God she would never see him again. Thank goodness, he had believed her claim that she had used him as a substitute for her lover, but that had only been in the shock of the moment, when his brain had been confused by the arousal of his body. Later, when he had time to think . . . to question . . . Shaking her head, she got up again. She couldn't stay up here. If she did, Mamie would come up, wanting to know what was wrong. She would have to go back down.

She was half-way across the hall when she bumped into Paul, walking the other way.

'Ah, there you are! Ma has just sent me to look for you.'

Susannah let him take her arm. Several people were milling about around the entrance to the marquee but, when Paul stopped, her glance went instinctively to the tall, dark-haired man with his back to her. Her heart started pumping frantically, her body shaking.

'Good, there's Hazard. He made it, after all. I'd better introduce him to Ma and Pop.'

'Hazard?' Susannah queried faintly.

'Yes. Hazard Maine. He and I both did a stint in Sydney. I met him a few months ago, and then we bumped into one another on the Qantas flight coming over. He's taking up a new post in this country and he's at a bit of a loose end. He was at school over here, apparently. He's lost touch with people since, and so I invited him here.'

'Where . . . where is he?'

'Over there.'

She stared, dumbstruck, at the dark head he was pointing out to her, and an appalling awareness of what she had done swept over her. The man who had accused her of having a married lover, the man she had let caress and arouse her in a way that no man had ever done, the man she had quite deliberately allowed to believe she was the very worst kind of hardened tramp, was Hazard Maine. Paul's friend . . . her new boss!

She made a small, inarticulate little sound of despair in her throat.

'Something wrong?'

'Paul . . . I . . . I have to go and talk to Richard,' she invented. 'I've just remembered something I should have told him.'

'Richard?' Paul called queryingly after her, but she was already disappearing into the crowd, and so he shrugged his shoulders and went on alone.

Hazard Maine! How could fate have tricked her so cruelly? Why had she not had any intuitive warning? Not even his accent had betrayed him. She had never imagined—never dreamed . . . She wondered frantically whether it was possible to change her whole appearance before Monday, whether she could somehow make herself unrecognisable. Then logic intruded, and she squared her shoulders.

There was nothing he could do. He could hardly sack her because she had allowed him a few physical intimacies, or because she had implied that she was simply using him to satisfy a need aroused by another man. No, he could hardly sack her for that, not without making himself look a fool, and Hazard Maine had not struck her as the type of man who welcomed being made to look a fool.

No, like her, he would just have to accept their working relationship.

And yet, reassure herself as she might, nothing could completely dispel her fear. It was too late now to regret her folly. And Aunt Emily hadn't brought her up to run away from life's problems. Besides, where could she run to? No, she would just have to brazen it out.

Brazen... She couldn't have chosen a more appropriate word, Susannah thought despairingly, remembering the taunting challenge she had flung in Hazard's face.

CHAPTER THREE

'COME on, Susannah. It's lunch time.'

Abruptly, Susannah came out of her reverie. All weekend, the awful coincidence of Paul knowing Hazard Maine and, worse still, of him inviting him to his parents' party, had preyed on her mind.

She had been right to dread meeting him again. It had lived up to her worst expectations. She had had to sit there in the full glare of his contempt, inwardly writhing with humiliation, while outwardly trying to appear calm and unmoved.

'Lizzie, I honestly don't think I want any lunch today.'

There was a moment's silence, and then the other girl said shrewdly, 'Why? Because Hazard singled you out at this morning's briefing? Don't be an idiot. If you don't turn up at the wine bar, the others are bound to guess why. This business isn't exactly running over with the milk of human kindness. I sometimes think that compassion is something that ceases to exist the moment anyone starts working in the media. If you miss out this lunch time, they're all going to guess why.'

Lizzie was right, of course. But it was her fierce outburst that caught Susannah's attention, more than what she had actually said. Lizzie had already been working as Richard's secretary when she herself had arrived. Normally, she was so quiet and placid, the kind of girl who preferred to keep herself very much to herself, and as she was not on the editorial staff in a reporting capacity she normally held aloof from any wrangles that broke out. And then Susannah remembered hearing that Lizzie's ex-husband had been a reporter on one of the television news programmes, and that he had left her for a colleague.

And Lizzie was quite right, of course. The others *would* all guess immediately what was wrong if she ducked out of lunch.

'I'll just get my coat.'

'And your umbrella,' Lizzie warned her. 'It's raining again.'

They had never had such a wet summer. Soon it would be autumn. A tiny shiver ran across Susannah's skin. Would all her hopes for the future and her career, hopes which had seemed so bright under Richard's benevolent eye, fade with the dying season? But why should Hazard Maine sit in judgement over her? *He* had been all too willing to take what he thought was on offer.

Use your brains, she derided herself as she followed Lizzie out on to the wet street. The fact that he wanted you, even momentarily, will make him resent you all the more.

'Hey, come on, we're here,' Lizzie reminded her, giving her a small push in the direction of the basement wine bar the magazine staff favoured for their lunch-time and after-work gatherings.

The rest of the crowd was already there—a noisy, cheerful bunch who drew amused and occasionally disapproving glances from the other lunch-time diners.

A small silence fell as Susannah walked in, and she mentally thanked Lizzie for making her come.

'Come on, have a pew,' someone called out. 'We were just bemoaning our collective fate. It seems our new boss is no Richard.'

'Yeah, that was some grilling he gave you this morning, Susie.'

She hated having her name abbreviated, but for once she forbore to comment, smiling vaguely in the direction of the speaker, and then shrugging her shoulders carelessly.

'What did you do?' someone else asked.

'Nothing, as far as I know. Perhaps he just doesn't like red hair.'

It was the best thing she could do on the spur of the moment, but it drew several appreciative laughs, and to her relief her colleagues' attention was drawn away from her by Claire, who announced drawlingly, 'Well, children, I'm afraid I must leave you. I've got to finish my column this afternoon, and I'm due at a society bash tonight. However, before I leave, I will give you all one word of warning. Be careful with our new boss, because rumour hath it that he's tipped to become chairman of the whole group when Mac retires.'

Mac was the term by which they all knew the chairman and owner of MacFarlane Publications, Tom MacFarlane, and in the storm of questions that followed Claire's announcement Susannah sat back to dwell silently on what she had said.

No one disputed her information. All of them knew that when Claire made that sort of statement she was invariably right.

'But what about Richard?' someone commented at last. 'Surely, as Caroline's husband ...'

'Oh, Richard ... A nice guy, but hardly corporate king-pin material,' Claire announced dismissively. 'No, it's definitely going to be Hazard. I got all the gen from a friend of mine who used to work with him.'

'But how do you know?' someone queried, obviously exasperated by her superior air.

'I have my sources. For instance, how many of you know, I wonder, that Hazard Maine's father was in partnership with Mac at one time?'

None of them, obviously.

'Well, he was, and then for some reason the partnership was dissolved, but our Mr Maine has always been pretty close to Mac. Practically like a son to him, apparently.'

'I wonder how Richard feels about that,' someone commented, and instantly, before she could prevent herself, Susannah leapt to her ex-boss's defence.

'Richard won't mind. He's not like that ...'

'Unfortunately for you.'

There was an ominous silence before Claire said lightly, 'Well, darling, as Richard's favourite protégée, let's face it, there could have been virtually no limit to the giddy heights to which you could have risen if he had been ambitious. Right to the very top, perhaps.'

Susannah wasn't sure if she liked what Claire was saying, but she held her tongue, knowing how her colleague loved to stir up trouble.

'Richard was very kind to me,' she agreed calmly.

One of the men, she wasn't sure which one, remarked *sotto voce*, 'I wonder why?' But once he realised she wasn't going to rise to the bait, he dropped the subject, and started talking instead about Hazard's likely changes to the magazine.

Susannah didn't enjoy the lunch she had ordered, but she forced herself to eat it, and gradually found herself relaxing slightly. No one really knew much about Hazard Maine, and she contented herself with listening to her colleague's comments about him.

Thankfully, none of them realised that there was more to his dislike of her than appeared on the surface; they were all taking his antipathy at face value, and it seemed to be the general consensus of opinion that it was caused by the fact that she had been Richard's favourite protégée.

'Don't worry,' one of her older male colleagues told her comfortingly as they returned to the office, 'once he gets hold of something he can really get his teeth into, he'll forget all about you. The trouble with these ex-newspaper men is that none of them can really ever accept that a magazine can be worthwhile editing. And you can bet that he's none too pleased about being landed with the job, no matter how rich the silver spoon it came on.'

As they walked back into the foyer, Lizzie glanced at her watch. 'I must go,' she apologised. 'Hazard has a very full afternoon. Planning meetings and goodness knows what.'

Which at least meant that *she* was hardly likely to see him again that day, Susannah thought thankfully as she sat down at her desk.

For the last few weeks, she had been painstakingly building up a file on a new author who had burst on the literary scene several months previously. No one had been allowed to interview him. He lived almost like a recluse, apparently, in some remote part of Yorkshire, and the only facts the media had on him were those grudgingly released by his publishers when it became clear that his book was going to be a runaway success.

It would be a wonderful coup for her if she could secure an interview with him, and at the moment she was engaged in very delicate negotiations with his publishers to that end.

She was lucky enough to have a contact within the publishing house itself—a fellow graduate who had actually met and knew the author.

'He's adamant that he doesn't want to get caught up in a publicity merry-go-round, but I'll do my best for you.'

Ever since she had come to work on the magazine, Susannah had never had a direct boss, reporting only to Richard, who allowed her to organise her own projects. She preferred working that way. She enjoyed the independence it gave her. She was deeply engrossed in her work when her internal telephone rang, and she cursed as she picked up the receiver.

To hear Lizzie's quiet voice on the other end of the line was the last thing she had expected, and her stomach muscles tensed anxiously as the other girl said apologetically, 'Susannah, Hazard wants to see you in his office right away.'

Never once in all the time she had worked for him had she ever received that sort of summons from Richard, but it was no use comparing the two men; there was no comparison.

Feeling appallingly nervous, but determined not to let it show, Susannah made her way down the corridor. The sight of Lizzie's head bent over her typewriter as she walked into the office didn't do anything to relieve her anxiety. Not quite able to meet her eyes, Lizzie motioned her towards the inner door.

'You're to go straight in.'

What on earth was she so frightened of? Susannah asked herself as she did as she was instructed. The worst he could do would be to sack her. Sack her... When she thought of how long she had had to wait for this opportunity! To lose her job now, when the employment market was so depressed; to be branded as a failure, which she would be...

It gave her an uncontrollable jolt to see the dark head bent over some papers, she was so used to seeing Richard sitting in that chair. Hazard didn't lift his head and, mindful of office etiquette, Susannah didn't sit down. He was signing something, letters it looked like, and she had to grit her teeth to stop herself from screaming out loud with the tension building up inside her. He was doing it deliberately, of course. Well, she would show him that she was indifferent to such treatment!

When at last he deigned to raise his head and look at her, she was proud of the calm, unconcerned way in which she was able to meet his scrutiny.

He was looking at her as though he found her in some way offensive, she realised with inner bitterness, but beneath the veneer of acid contempt she could just glimpse a darker, deeper anger.

This was a man of intense male energy and pride, and *she* had challenged that pride, had touched it where it was perhaps most vulnerable, she acknowledged. Although he didn't look like a man who was in any way sexually vulnerable, he must be, otherwise surely he would never have been so angry.

Wouldn't he? Would any human being relish being told that they were simply being used as a sexual object? She shivered a little. It was too late to regret that now. Not for the first time in her life, Susannah inwardly cursed her own impulsiveness. This wasn't the first unpleasant situation it had led her into, but it was certainly going to be the worst.

'Sit down.'

It wasn't a request but a command, and Susannah stiffened instinctively, resisting the harsh voice.

'Are you aurally, as well as morally deficient, Miss Hargreaves?'

The acid words were spoken softly, each one tipped with deliberate venom, and Susannah had opened her mouth to cry out a furious denial before she realised that this man standing in front of her was her boss and not merely another colleague.

Mutely seething with resentment, she sat down.

'Excellent. Now that I have had a chance to assimilate how this magazine is run, I intend to institute some changes. One of these will be that, from now on, you will be working as my assistant.'

His assistant!

She was too shocked to give voice to the objections clamouring for utterance, but her white face and furious eyes gave her away.

'Try not to think of it as a demotion so much as as a sideways move,' suggested Hazard with soft malice.

A demotion! Her brain reeled. Of course... In the shock of hearing his first words, all she had been able to think of was her own reaction to working in close proximity to him.

A demotion! Fierce heat scalded her skin.

'My work!'

'Your work is something I am having rather a problem in assessing, Miss Hargreaves,' he told her bluntly, and from beneath the pile of letters he removed a folder.

'In here are the articles you have done while working for the magazine. Very good, well thought-out and rational articles, which more often than not betray a partisanship and compassion for the, shall we say, more unfortunate victims of our society than I would have expected from—er—a woman of your ilk. In short, Miss Hargreaves, I suspect that *your* articles can, in fact, be more properly attributed elsewhere.'

What was he saying? Susannah could barely take it all in. Was he actually suggesting that someone else had written her work? But...

She was too stunned to defend herself.

'I know, of course, that you were Richard's protégée...'

'And you think that Richard wrote my articles?' she interrupted wildly, instantly seeing where his words were leading.

'What I think or suspect is not primarily at issue,' he told her smoothly. 'For the good of the magazine as a whole, I can hardly allow you to work unchecked until I have resolved my doubts as to your ability, and it is for that reason that I have decided that, from now on, you will work as my assistant.'

'Editing *your* features,' Susannah guessed bitterly. 'Aren't you afraid I might pirate them and sell them to someone else?'

The smile he gave her made her toes curl in apprehension.

'Why don't you try it?' he suggested softly. 'But, before you do, let me warn you that I'd love a legitimate reason for getting rid of you.'

The reality of what was happening to her hit her like a bucket of icy water. She couldn't afford to lose this job, she acknowledged with a sense of panic. The media world was a notoriously small one. It loved nothing better than to gossip. *Tomorrow* was the very best magazine of its kind on the market. If she lost her job here... She shivered suddenly and then tensed, seeing Hazard Maine's frown, not knowing it had been caused by the vulnerability of her mouth and eyes.

'As from tomorrow morning, you'll be working in here. It's all arranged. Your desk will be moved tonight and, as soon as the morning conference is over, I'll want to go over with you all the projects you're presently working on.'

He bent his head back over the papers on his desk, and Susannah didn't know whether she was supposed to stay or go. Every muscle in her body seemed to be seized in a peculiar sort of paralysis. It was the shock, she told herself.

The dark head lifted, icy grey eyes studying her.

'What are you waiting for, Miss Hargreaves?'

Somehow, she managed to get herself out of the office, thankful to discover that Lizzie wasn't sitting at her desk. Fate seemed to relent a little as she hurried back to her own cubby-hole, because she got there without seeing anyone.

Once there, she sank down into her chair, simply staring into space as she tried to come to grips with what had happened. It seemed impossible that Hazard Maine had actually accused her of putting her name to work done by someone else. Surely he knew Richard would never have countenanced it, for one thing? Why hadn't she said that to him? she wondered, shivering with reaction. Why had she just sat there like a dumb bunny, taking everything he had chosen to fling at her?

She could hardly march back into his office and tell him now. If she wanted to keep her job, she would just have to prove to him how wrong he was. Oh, but it was so unfair! *Life* was so unfair, she thought bitterly, only too relieved to see that it was well gone five, and that she could leave.

Of course, she would have to run into Hazard just as she was crossing the foyer, all wrapped up in her raincoat

'Leaving already?' he taunted, glancing up at the clock. 'Make the most of it, Miss Hargreaves, because from tomorrow you're going to discover what work is really all about.'

Half-way through the evening, just as she was finishing off a thank-you letter to Mamie, who was very keen on such matters, her telephone rang.

She stared at it for several seconds, frowning. Only a few people had her number here at the flat. One of them was David, and she was shocked to discover how much she dreaded the thought of picking up the receiver and hearing his voice.

She had been in love with the idea of love, she admitted wearily, reaching for it. For the man himself, she had no feelings left at all, other than those of distaste for what he had done to his wife, and resentment over the way he had tried to use her.

'Susannah, is that you?'

It took her several minutes to place the female voice, and then her brain cleared and she recognised it.

'Nicky!'

'I thought you might like to hear the latest on John Howard.'

John Howard was the author Susannah was hoping to interview. Her interview with Hazard had driven all thoughts of him out of her mind.

'Listen, I think he might be weakening. He was here on Friday and I talked to him and ... Susannah, are you still there?'

Hurriedly assuring her friend that she was indeed listening, Susannah tried to banish Hazard from her mind. He had told her that from now on she would be working only as his assistant on projects selected by him. No doubt Hazard Maine, with his background of war correspondence, would find something like interviewing an elusive top-selling author boring and mundane. No doubt he would prefer something like in-depth reporting on a terrorist group.

'I ...'

'Look,' Nicky said impatiently, 'John stayed over in London this weekend, and I've managed to get him to agree to meet you. That's why I'm ringing. Can you make it for dinner at the Connaught this evening?'

Dinner at the Connaught! Susannah's imagination boggled slightly.

As though she found her silence exasperating, Nicky demanded impatiently, 'Well, can you make it or not?'

'Yes—yes, I can make it. What time?'

She had rung off before she had clearly realised that she ought to have informed Nicky that the whole project was probably now in abeyance. But she had been pursuing the interview for so long, she was reluctant to back out now, when she was potentially so close to success.

She dressed carefully for the meeting. Clothes which were too elegant or aggressive would be bound to put him off. Interviewees always regarded interviewers in much the same vein as a torture victim did his tormentor, she knew that; and yet the Connaught . . . she could hardly appear in her jeans and sweatshirt!

In the end, she settled for the plain black silk dress which had been Mamie's Christmas present to her. It was fitted and yet feminine in design without being overtly sexy. The soft black fabric enhanced the delicacy of her skin. Black had always been one of her colours, but the air of fragility reflected back to her by her mirror irritated her.

It was impossible that she had lost weight since this morning, but surely her face looked thinner and slightly more fine-drawn? Her eyes seemed almost haunted, and her mouth.

Cross with herself, Susannah turned away from the mirror. She was an idiot to let Hazard Maine affect her like this. Richard had warned her more than once that she needed to toughen up, and she had always accepted that he was right. She loved her work, but sometimes she hated the cynicism that seemed to go hand in hand with it.

She arrived dead on time and, following Nicky's instructions, asked to be shown to the bar.

It wasn't too crowded and she saw her friend immediately. Of John Howard, there was no sign.

Nicky was seated with an older woman, who looked slightly apprehensive, and politely Susannah quelled her disappointment. Perhaps the writer had changed his mind. It was only when she saw that he wasn't present that she realised how much she had been looking forward to meeting him, and not just because of the potential interview. She had read his book and loved it, amazed and awed by the degree of compassion he had shown, not just for his male but also for his female characters.

Swallowing her disappointment, she smiled warmly both at Nicky and her companion.

The older woman smiled back. She was about fifty, with elegantly styled hair and a face which portrayed a strong character.

Politeness forbade Susannah from making any comment on the missing author. She had obviously arrived just as Nicky and her companion were deep in discussion, and Susannah sat back, waiting until they had finished.

The look that Nicky exchanged with the older woman puzzled her, until Nicky said calmly, 'Susannah, I'd like you to meet Emma King, otherwise known as John Howard!'

'John Howard!' Susannah's eyes widened as she betrayed her surprise. Of course, this wasn't the first time a writer had hidden behind a false name, or indeed adopted one that belonged to the opposite sex, but somehow she had never envisaged John Howard as a woman.

She said so quite openly, and was rewarded with a pleased smile.

'And therein, I'm afraid, lies my dilemma. I've just put the finishing touches to a novel that continues where *Past Times* leaves off, and I'm concerned that if my identity is revealed then it will affect the book's reception.'

'Emma feels that the publishing world is still very much a male bastion, and that female writers are sometimes treated badly. She prefers to preserve her male identity as far as the media are concerned because she feels that, once she's reviewed as a female writer, her work won't get the same sort of serious consideration that it does now.'

Susannah could understand what she meant and she frowned, her quick brain searching for a solution while she heard Emma saying quietly, 'I've always refused to give any interviews, but I was so impressed by the articles you've done, and by what Nicky had to say about you, that I decided to make an exception in your case. But you can see my dilemma. If I allow you to do an interview...'

'If *you* allowed me to do one, yes,' Susannah agreed quickly. 'But I shouldn't be interviewing Emma King, I should be interviewing John Howard.'

For a moment, both her listeners looked bewildered.

'Look,' she explained quickly, 'as far as the public is concerned, John Howard is the author of *Past Times*, and it's John Howard in whom they're interested.'

'You mean, I could give the interview as though I were, in fact, a man?' Emma asked, catching on. 'But wouldn't that be dishonest?'

'Not necessarily. It depends on the line the interview takes. At *Tomorrow*, our line would be on your writing. We don't go in for revelations about people's lives. Our interview would be conducted on the basis of your work as a writer. What made you want to write, how you got started...that sort of thing.'

'Well, if you think we could pull it off...' Doubt was giving way to interest. 'Look, I need to think about it,' Emma told her. 'I'm going home tomorrow morning. Why don't I give you a ring, and then, if I'm prepared to go ahead, we could fix another meeting?'

Susannah didn't push for any more concessions, her brain was still striving to assimilate what it had already learned.

Over dinner, she discovered a little more about the elusive writer, and she tingled with the excitement that was her writer's intuition and which told her that, if she could just gain her trust, in Emma she would find an interviewee who would give her an article that was well worth having.

It was late when she finally got up from the table, exclaiming ruefully that she had better leave. Nicky was staying on with Emma to discuss some mutual points of business and, as she made her way through the now busy dining-room, Susannah had the feeling that someone was watching her.

She paused to allow a waiter to manoeuvre a bulky sweet trolley and the sensation intensified. She could almost feel two eyes burning into the back of her head. It was an uncanny sensation, and one that was rather alien to her.

Willing herself not to turn round, she hurried to the exit, but a couple leaving a table ahead of her blocked the way, and the woman turned abruptly, almost knocking her over and causing her to spin.

It was as she straightened up that she saw him. He was seated at a table only feet away from her, his grey eyes blazing contempt and something else that made her shudder uncontrollably, her flesh flooded with sensual heat as, against her will, she was forced to recall those moments when his mouth had touched her skin.

Hazard, here... He was like some malign fate, blocking her every path. She had a muzzy impression of the group seated with him: one of them was a blonde who looked slightly petulant at not being the whole focus of his attention—just his type, thought Susannah acidly as she deliberately turned her back without acknowledging him.

As she got into a taxi, she told herself that she wasn't going to allow him to disrupt what little peace of mind she had left. She might have to endure his presence during working hours, but once outside work she was going to blank him out of her consciousness completely.

She succeeded, but she had forgotten about her subconscious, and her dreams were filled with vivid images of him, with memories of the sensual sensations conjured up by his hands and his mouth.

She woke up twice, her body damp with sweat, her stomach muscles cramping denyingly against the dull ache of desire spreading through her lower body. She hated him and he hated her, but she couldn't deny that physically he aroused her. Somehow she was going to have to come to terms with that unpalatable fact.

CHAPTER FOUR

'HEY, Susie, what's all this about your desk being moved into Hazard's office?'

Susannah stopped, uncomfortably aware of the calculating curiosity in Jim Neaves' eyes.

Jim had tried to date her when she'd first joined the magazine. Hurting from the realisation that David had not been honest and open with her, she had been in no mood for Jim's blatantly motivated advances, and now she admitted that perhaps she had not let him down as tactfully as she might.

'I . . .'

'From now on, Susannah will be working as my assistant.'

Hazard's clipped, impatient voice made them both start. Jim considered himself something of a high-flyer and the equal of any man born, not to mention the superior of most of the female sex, and yet almost instantly he heard Hazard's voice his manner became embarrassingly servile.

'*Another* of your admirers, is he?' Hazard drawled when he had gone. 'Perhaps there's something I should make clear to you. I don't care what kind of kiss-and-tease games you've been playing around here in the past, from now on they're going to stop.'

Susannah was completely lost for words. There was no way she could defend herself without referring to that dreadful weekend at Mamie's, and that was the last thing she wanted to do. If she explained to him that she wasn't what he thought, he might start wondering *why* she had been so determined that he should believe that she was substituting him for her non-existent married lover, and that was a question she wasn't sure she could answer herself yet.

Lizzie was bent over her typewriter, fingers flying as Susannah walked through her office. Deliberately? Very probably, Susannah thought miserably, remembering the other girl's sensitivity towards the feelings of others. She must have heard what Hazard had said to her.

It was a shock to walk into Hazard's office and discover that her desk, far from being set up in a corner, had been aligned at a right angle to his own, and her terminal and word processor already installed.

From that position, he would be able to reach out and look at what she was doing. The thought unnerved her.

The outer door opened and she lifted her eyes from her desk. Unlike most of the other men working on the magazine, Hazard favoured formal office wear, and his restrained dark suit emphasised the lean arrogance of his body. The sensual contrast between the dark tanned skin and the whiteness of his shirt cuffs made an unwanted frisson of awareness wash through her, leaving her tense.

'Sit down,' he commanded brusquely. 'You're not back at school.'

Just managing to subdue the belligerent comment burning her tongue, Susannah fiddled with some of the things on her desk, deliberately remaining standing. From beneath her lashes, she sent him a glowering look of dislike.

The outer door opened and Lizzie called out, 'Coffee, Hazard?'

'Please.'

'And you, Susannah?'

'She can get her own.'

Flushing with mortification, Susannah stared fiercely at her desk, willing the bright sparkle of angry tears in her eyes to clear before she lifted her head. When she did so, Lizzie had gone.

After that, she deliberately waited until Hazard had gone into his morning meeting with the heads of departments before going to get her coffee. The rich smell of his as it had stood on his desk had driven her mad with longing, but she had been determined not to give way in front of him.

Lizzie, tactful as a good secretary always should be, said nothing when she saw her coming back holding the plastic cup, other than a calm, 'Another miserable day. If this is summer, give me winter!'

'Umm... I heard on the news this morning that several areas are being threatened with floods.'

Her aunt's home in Leicestershire was in a small village in a very flat, exposed part of the county, and concern for her made Susannah impulsively pick up the telephone. Personal telephone calls were frowned upon officially, but in practice Richard had always turned a blind eye to the odd call, and she had never been the type of person to abuse any kind of privilege. It was just that she knew that Aunt Emily normally played bridge on Monday evenings, and then liked to go to bed early, so if Susannah wanted to be sure of speaking to her, it would be as well for her to ring now.

She answered the call on the fourth ring, and assured Susannah that there was no cause for concern. The river had risen, but not too dramatically and there was no immediate danger.

Speaking to her, Susannah could picture the old lady, with her tight bun and her shrewd blue eyes. Her childhood with Emily had not been an easy one, and certainly materially it had not been a rich one, but there were other forms of richness. All those long walks with Aunt Emily painstakingly pointing out the names of wild flowers and small animals; those long dark evenings spent learning to knit and sew, and then later to play the piano while the majority of her peers watched television. Then there had been expeditions in the autumn to pick berries, which were later turned into jams and preserves. Aunt Emily preferred to bake her own bread, and Susannah had been taught all the arts of a careful housewife from a very young age.

She was just replacing the receiver when Hazard walked in, and she knew without reading it in his face that she looked a picture of guilt. She had never ever been any good at deception, and as he watched her she felt herself flushing uncomfortably.

'A personal call, I presume?' he said softly, looking from her flushed face to the receiver she was just replacing.

'Yes . . . Yes. It was . . . Richard . . .'

She knew the moment she said Richard's name that she had made a mistake. It was an effort not to let herself flinch under the freezingly bitter look Hazard gave her.

'God, you never stop, do you? Have you *no* conscience? No awareness of what you're doing? Or is it just that you know, but you damn well don't care?'

He was standing beside her desk, towering over her, and for one moment Susannah thought he was actually going to reach down and drag her to her feet.

As she trembled in fright and resentment, his telephone rang. For a moment she thought he was actually going to ignore it. Then, with a frown, he turned away and she was able to relax.

She couldn't help help overhearing his conversation, or recognising the voice of the woman on the other end.

So Claire had been right, and Hazard did know Caroline and her father. Susannah had met Richard's wife on several occasions and had quite liked her. In her middle thirties, she was a self-assured, rather brittle-looking brunette who was very much the dominant partner in the marriage.

Richard seemed to adore her, and that was one of the things Susannah had liked most about him.

'Right,' Hazard began again when he had finished his phone call. 'I want...'

He frowned as the telephone rang again. Hers this time, and Susannah froze with fury and disbelief as he stopped her from answering it, picking up the receiver himself.

He listened for a few seconds, his frown deepening all the time, and then handed the receiver over to her. 'It's John Howard's secretary for you. She wants to confirm a time and place for your interview.'

Her heart thumping uncomfortably, Susannah took the receiver from him. She realised the moment the 'secretary' spoke that it was Emma, but when it became clear that Emma wanted her to go to Yorkshire the following week to interview her on her home ground, Susannah had to back-pedal slightly.

'The dates you've given me seem fine,' she told her. 'But I'll have to check with my boss. Can I come back to you?'

'John Howard?' Hazard queried when she had finished her call. 'Is that John Howard, the writer?'

'Yes... An old friend of mine works for his publisher, and managed to set up a meeting for me... I... It's something I've been working towards for a while.'

'So why the delay in arranging an interview, or was that just to make the poor guy sweat a little? I suppose a woman like you can't help but play with them, even in a work context.'

For once, she was immune to his contempt, temper making her eyes darken as the pupils enlarged with emotion.

'You couldn't be more wrong. What I said was the truth. I have to check with you before I can do the interview. You said that from now on I was working as your assistant, remember?'

'Don't try getting round me,' came back the cynical retort. 'It won't work. I've seen the real you. It would be quite a scoop for us if we can pull the interview off,' he continued, 'although I must say I'm not convinced that you're the right person to do it. This friend you mentioned... a man, no doubt?'

'No, as a matter of fact, a woman,' Susannah told him sweetly, with a great deal of satisfaction.

'Give me John Howard's number. I'll give him a ring and sort something out. I could even do the interview myself at a pinch.'

How she managed to control her temper, Susannah didn't know. How dared he calmly appropriate all her hard work, and then deny her the right to complete it? She thought about keeping the fact that John Howard was in fact Emma King to herself, and then thought better of it. Her loyalty to the magazine and the ethic she had been brought up with would not allow her to be so underhand. She might not get her name beneath the interview, but she would hate the magazine to lose it altogether because she hadn't been able to resist the temptation to outwit Hazard Maine. And it *was* a temptation!

'There's just one thing you should know first.' Reluctantly, she told him the whole story, outlining the basis on which the interview had been agreed.

'Why are you telling me this?' he asked her when she had finished. There was a rather odd look in his eyes, and his mouth curled down, as though he had been forced to taste something unpleasant. As, no doubt, humble pie was to a man of his arrogant pride, Susannah thought angrily.

'Because if I don't, we, as a magazine, could possibly lose the whole interview,' she told him succinctly.

His eyebrows rose. 'My goodness! Altruism? Forgive me if I find it suspect.'

Her temper broke its bond. No one in her life had treated her like this, and it was fraying her nerves and wearing her down to the point where she was beyond heeding the warnings of caution.

'Why are you treating me like this? What have I done to...'

'What have you done? My God, how can you dare to ask me that? Do you really want me to spell it out for you? All right then I will. You looked at me like a lonely lost soul. You let me kiss you, touch you like you'd been waiting for me all your life, and then you turn round and tell me that it's all an act. That you don't want *me* at all...that I'm just filling in for someone else. A woman who can do that to a man, any man, is capable of anything.'

And there was no way she was going to be able to change his mind. Not without letting him know far more about her life than she wanted him to know.

'Just what kind of woman are you?' he continued fiercely. 'You break up someone's marriage, not caring what you're doing, and then; when your lover neglects you to be with his wife, you coldly and callously...' He shook his head, not finishing the sentence. 'There's no one I despise more than a marriage breaker, of either sex.'

'You think we can all choose with whom we become emotionally involved?' Susannah demanded. 'You must have very strong will-power, never to have been tempted yourself.'

Later she would be shocked at her folly in challenging him like this, but right now nothing mattered other than not allowing him to trample all over her.

'Oh, I've been tempted.' The explicit look he gave her made her skin burn and her heart beat in shallow, nervy little thuds. 'I've just made sure that I've never given *in* to that temptation. I try to take a longer view of the situation. A woman who'll leave her husband for me, sooner or later might, potentially, leave me for someone else.'

'Lucky you, you can control who you are and aren't attracted to,' Susannah came back acidly.

'I didn't say that. Perhaps I *am* just lucky. Quite frankly, the thought of a married woman going behind her husband's back to sleep with me turns me off.'

'Lucky or cold-blooded,' Susannah muttered as she bent her head over her work, unwilling to admit that he had got the best of her, and the worst thing was that really she agreed with every single word he had said.

How on earth had she got herself into this muddle? It was too late now to back down and plead for a second chance. And, besides, why should she care what he thought of her?

She had to leave the office to check on some information, and when she came back Hazard was just putting down the telephone receiver.

'We're going to Yorkshire a week on Friday to do the Howard interview,' he told her coolly.

'Both of us?'

His mouth thinned.

'It seems John Howard won't hear of it being done without you.'

It was plain that he wasn't pleased, but neither was she. The last thing she wanted to do was to be thrust into his company for an entire day.

'We'll need to get an early start. I'll pick you up at half-past seven. Where do you live?'

Reluctantly she told him and then comforted herself with the reflection that the drive would be purgatory for him just as it would for her.

The phone rang again and, listening to Hazard as he dealt with one of their advertisers who should more properly have asked to speak to the head of the advertising department, Susannah felt grudging respect for him colouring her resentment.

It was no sinecure being the managing editor of a magazine like *Tomorrow*, where they carried no excess staff and where the pressure on whoever was at the helm was the greatest. Mac, as Tom MacFarlane was known irreverently by most of his employees, had no brief for time-wasters, and Richard had once confessed to her that he found his autocratic father-in-law hard work on occasions.

Another phone call at five past five took Hazard down to the art department. Half-way to the door, he called out to Susannah, 'You'd better come with me—oh, and bring a notebook.'

Her unruly tongue longed to remind him that *she* wasn't his secretary. In point of fact, Lizzie had already gone home, but caution prevailed.

She had had a hard time over lunch, ignoring her colleagues' curious questions about her new role. Pride would not allow her to admit that it was a demotion, and she had been astonished to discover how many of them envied her, thinking she had been picked out for special on-the-spot training.

'You'd better watch out,' Claire had remarked acidly. 'The next thing you know, you'll be sent out to Beirut.'

General laughter had greeted this sally, but privately Susannah had acknowledged that Beirut, or somewhere like it, probably was exactly where Hazard would like to send her, in the knowledge that she was extremely unlikely to survive!

Day succeeded day, and Susannah found that she was working harder than she had ever worked in her life. That did not surprise her; what did was her own reaction to the pressure Hazard put on her. There were times when she actually found she was enjoying her new role.

Hazard, it quickly became clear, took the 'managing' part of his title extremely seriously indeed, and now and again, on those rare occasions when she glimpsed grudging respect in his eyes, she felt as intoxicated as though she had drunk a whole bottle of champagne.

The others teased her unmercifully, accusing her of becoming a workaholic.

Her private life, never particularly hectic, had dwindled to nothing—there wasn't time. When she eventually got home from the magazine at night, she made copious notes of what she was learning, nearly always eating her supper while doing so. After that, she either read or listened to music for a couple of hours, and then she was in bed, ready for an early start the next day.

And yet, against all the odds, she found she was enjoying it. She had actually grown to relish her clashes with Hazard; just as long as she clung on to the memory of that hot, fierce flash of desire in his eyes the night they had met, she was immune to his sarcasm. It was like a charm protecting her.

Of course, he didn't desire her now, but that memory of his momentary weakness was like the sweetest pain-killer administered to her hurts.

And there *were* hurts: barbs flung with deadly accuracy that stung and stuck. But oddly enough they were never delivered in anyone else's presence, and to her surprise the rest of the staff continued to think that she was lucky in being singled out for special attention from their new boss.

'You'd better watch out,' one of them had told her. 'The next thing you know, he'll be trying to get you into his bed.'

'Susannah isn't Hazard's type,' Claire had interrupted.

'Then what is?' one of the junior receptionists, a pretty fluffy blonde, had quizzed her expectantly.

'Unmarried, or well divorced, round about thirty, intelligent, attractive, but most of all the type of woman who isn't looking for a husband,' Claire had told them. 'While he's involved with someone he's faithful to her, but his affairs are always pretty short-lived.'

'Nice work if you can get it,' one of them commented enviously, and the little blonde pouted and looked rather put out.

It was eight o'clock on Thursday evening when Hazard eventually announced that she could leave. With their early morning start for Yorkshire very much to the forefront of her mind, Susannah gritted her teeth and tried to conceal her irritation. She had to go home, wash her hair, lay her things out for the morning, then read up on her file one last time...

With her mind full of these and half a dozen other things, she was stunned to hear Hazard saying almost conversationally, 'You know, you're a very irritating contradiction, Susannah. These past few days, you've taken everything I've thrown at you without a murmur. You've worked hard and well.'

He was perched on the edge of his desk, and unwillingly her attention was caught by the taut muscles of his thighs. A curious sensation, not unlike a minor electric shock, galvanised her, an uncomfortable prickly awareness of him as a man. And it wasn't the first time since she'd started working for him that she had felt that awareness.

'Is there any rule that says I shouldn't?' she asked him flippantly, anxious to dispel the creeping sense of intimacy invading the room.

They were alone in his office, and the rest of the staff had long since gone home. Hazard had wanted to acquaint himself with all the personnel files and she had stayed behind to help him. Not strictly her job, but she had quickly learned that the more she protested the more he enjoyed her torment.

'No, but it seems out of character. Or are you trying to disarm me?'

'Why should I?'

'So that I'll stop keeping you late after work and you can go and meet your married lover,' he told her cynically. 'Five to seven *is* the favourite time for such meetings, isn't it? Before he has to go home to the country to join his wife and family.'

His cynicism infuriated her. She longed to hurl the truth at his arrogant head, but pride kept her silent. Pride and an increasingly intense feeling of self-preservation. It wouldn't do to have him probing too deeply into her motives for rejecting him the night they had met. She had lied to him then, and by keeping silent she had virtually lied to him ever since; she doubted that he would be very gentle with her if she admitted as much now. Her supposed married lover created a barrier between them; a barrier behind which she could hide...

The direction her errant thoughts moved in disturbed her. Why should she need such a barrier?

Out of the corner of her eye, she saw Hazard frown and look at his watch.

'Time to call it a day. I want to get home in time to catch the mid-evening news. That kidnap in Beirut...'

A war correspondent had been captured by one of the warring factions and was being held as a bargaining counter.

'Do you know him?'

She wasn't sure what had made her ask the quiet question. His compliment on her work must have weakened her defences, or perhaps it was because of the tiredness she could see in his eyes and the faint shadow that darkened them.

'Yes. We worked together some years back. He's a married man with two small kids. I'm godfather to one of them.' As she watched, he rubbed his temple as though it ached. 'I'll have to ring Jenny...'

Susannah had the impression that he had almost forgotten that she was there, and she wished she could just go quietly away without disturbing him. She felt like an intruder, the sensitive core of her personality touched by his concern for his friend's wife, and his friend's family, but instead she asked abruptly, 'Jenny?'

It was a mistake. He frowned and then focused on her as though he had forgotten for a moment that she was there. Immediately, the vulnerability vanished from his eyes, to be replaced by the hard glitter she had come to know and distrust. It was a warning to her that he was going to be at his most sardonically unkind.

'Ian's wife. The sort of wife any man would be proud of. A true woman in every sense of the word. Rather like Richard's wife, in fact. You do know Richard's wife, don't you?'

His tone was slightly hectoring, ugly almost, and Susannah was at a loss to understand why.

She stammered slightly as she responded uncertainly, 'Yes... Yes, I have met her. She seems very nice.'

She couldn't think of anything else to say, but his whole stance was so obviously that of a man awaiting a response that she felt obliged to say something.

His mouth twisted as though it were full of bitter aloes.

'Nice!' He gave a harsh laugh. 'I'm sure she'd be very pleased to hear that you think so.'

Susannah couldn't understand what they were doing talking about Richard's wife, but she had learned now to be wary when Hazard got into one of these bitter, angry moods. Sometimes she could almost see him checking himself, as though he was as astonished at the intensity of his anger towards her as she was herself.

'Just give me one good reason why a woman like you needs to demean herself by stealing someone else's husband,' he demanded suddenly. 'Just one.'

He seemed almost obsessed by her supposed relationship with a married man; more so, she sometimes thought, than with the brush-off she had given him. It was odd—it didn't fit in with the character she had given him, but then, nor did so many other things.

She had prepared herself for a battle over her promise that they would maintain Emma King's real identity, but to her surprise he had immediately and happily accepted that it should be so. On other occasions where she had expected him to show harshness and lack of understanding, he had caught her off guard with his compassionate acceptance of the frailties of others. So why did he continually come down so hard on her? She wasn't the first woman in the world to be stupid enough to fall for a married man.

Tell him that it's over, that it isn't what he thinks, an inner voice urged her, but how could she? It just wasn't possible.

'Nothing to say? The leopard never changes its spots, eh, Susannah, and that's what you are, isn't it? A beautiful predator!'

In that moment, looking up into his handsome, cynical face, Susannah wished that she might at least have the claws of the beast to whom he likened her! If she had, there was nothing she would like to do more than to rake them across that hard, tanned face.

The violence of her emotions shocked her. She turned away, her body shivering convulsively.

'What's the matter?' Hazard was at her elbow. She could feel his breath on the nape of her neck. It sent betraying shudders of sensation down her spine. Why, oh, why did she have to be so closely attuned to this man? That was what was at the root of her problem. That was the reason why she couldn't tell him the truth, and yet, working beside him, it was getting harder and harder to maintain the fiction of her married lover.

'You can't have been seeing much of him lately. I've been keeping you too busy. Missing him, are you, Susannah? Missing him in your bed?'

Her whole body was quivering now. She felt as though she was drowning in the soft whisper of his voice. A tormenting need to turn round and look at him swept through her.

'I'm not listening to this . . . I'm going home. I . . .' Wildly, she rushed to the door, not daring to look round. She could feel her face flaming with guilt and embarrassment. Just for a moment, a crazy, idiotic moment, she had actually felt weak at the knees, had actually mentally been picturing herself lying on some mythical bed, the shadowy figure of a nude male kneeling at her side. Such was the power of Hazard's masculinity.

To her relief he didn't follow her, simply calling after her, 'I'm going to make you give him up, Susannah.'

It stopped her in her tracks, her eyes huge and fearful as she turned to face him. She didn't doubt the truth of what he said, only the purpose behind him.

'Why?'

She hadn't realised she had whispered the word out loud until he crossed the space dividing them.

'Call it part of my one-man crusade against the destruction of the honourable state of marriage. Be warned. Whatever it takes, I'm going to stop it.'

His phone rang and, as he turned to answer it, she fled.

CHAPTER FIVE

SUSANNAH'S alarm woke her. She had been restless all night, falling asleep only a short time before dawn, and the intrusive shrill of the alarm made her groan protestingly until she realised what day it was.

Another hour and Hazard would be there. Scrambling out of bed, she headed for the shower.

The vibrant sting of its jets helped her to come to. Her hair, sleeked back with moisture, started to spring up in tendrils of curls as she rubbed it dry. No time to spend blowing and taming it this morning, she decided ruefully, pulling on a comfortable pair of worn jeans.

The radio announcer read the weather forecast. More rain, and it would be colder in the north; it was bound to be. A fine cotton shirt with a thick heavy sweatshirt to go over it would seem to be the most sensible thing to wear. Moisturiser to protect her skin, and the merest touch of make-up and she was ready— well, almost.

In her small kitchen, the coffee was filtering noisily, the rich scent of it making her mouth water. She was hopeless in the morning until she had had her first cup.

She wondered about making up a flask to take with her. Hazard had given her no indication of his plans for their journey. It would be a long drive, and if he decided not to stop—— She had a Thermos hidden away somewhere. She found it at the back of a cup-board and emerged breathless and triumphant, quickly washing it out and then filling it with the fragrant hot brew.

The radio announced the time; if she was quick, she would just be able to manage a slice of toast. As she made it, she looked out of the window and down on to the landscaped parking area she shared with the other residents. There was no sign of Hazard as yet.

She had been lucky to find this flat. When she had first come to London, she had visions of having to live in some small bedsit but, once she knew of her niece's decision to move to the capital, Aunt Emily had astounded her by informing her that she had kept for her the money realised from the sale of her parents' home at the time of their death, and that this sum, carefully invested and nurtured, had grown into a very healthy amount, enough to enable her to buy this flat, and to afford her small second-hand car as well.

The block was one of several built on land which had once housed a large Victorian villa. The estab-lished trees around the perimeter had been retained, and the flats were in the main owned by older retired couples. Susannah had decorated hers herself when she'd first moved in—it had been a way of passing those long sleepless hours when she had been strug-gling to come to terms with the fact that her rela-tionship with David was over.

Her kitchen was painted sunny yellow, and pretty candy-striped Austrian blinds decorated the windows. She had made them herself—thanks to Aunt Emily's careful training.

Her toaster, often erratic, started to billow smoke, and with a wail of protest she left the window and rushed over to it. By the time she had unplugged it and rescued the burnt bread, she was cursing mildly. The knock on her outer door made her stiffen and glance instinctively towards the window.

Down in the car park stood a long, lean, black Jaguar.

She hadn't wanted Hazard to come up to the flat; she had intended to run down and meet him the moment she saw his car, but it was too late now.

Crossly she went to open the door. Like herself, he was dressed casually, his jeans—like hers—well worn and faded. Against her will, Susannah's eyes were drawn to the way they hugged the hard muscles of his thighs. Grateful of the dimness of the hall for hiding the betraying colour sweeping up under her skin, she gestured to him to come in.

'I'm almost ready, I'll just get my jacket.'

To her annoyance, instead of remaining in the hall, he followed her down the passage and into the kitchen.

'Trouble with the toaster?' he asked as the acrid scent of the burnt bread met him.

He looked at the coffee machine and added, 'I don't suppose, if I ask very nicely, I'll be given a cup of that, will I?'

What could she do? Grimly, she got a mug and poured a cup for him.

It disconcerted her how at home he looked here in her kitchen. He had pulled out one of the stools from the wall, and was perching on it, looking out of the window.

'Nice place you've got here.'

'Yes,' Susannah agreed, 'and before you say it, no, it wasn't paid for by my lover. I bought it myself with an inheritance.'

'Quite a considerable inheritance,' he concurred mildly, getting up to touch one of her striped blinds. 'These things don't come cheap.'

'I made them myself.'

She had said it stiffly, angry and defensive with him, and also, if she was honest with herself, disturbed by his presence here in the intimacy of her kitchen. She wasn't used to sharing her morning routine with anyone, much less a man, and the sight of him prowling round her kitchen, studying it, disconcerted her.

'We ought to leave,' she reminded him. 'The traffic...'

'Yes.' He saw the Thermos and his eyebrows lifted interrogatively.

'I wasn't sure whether you planned to stop on the way,' she explained. 'I'd filled the filter jug, so...'

'Good idea. We'll probably need it if the weather report is anything to go by.' He saw her uncomprehending look and told her, 'I rang up the weather centre before I left. They're forecasting torrential rain and high-speed winds for Yorkshire today and tomorrow.'

He had finished his coffee, and she picked up his mug and her own, taking them over to the sink. Aunt Emily's training dictated that she left the kitchen immaculate, and she had long ago developed a morning routine that included this chore. However, she was totally thrown when Hazard, after watching her run the water and fill the washing-up bowl, said casually, 'Where's the tea towel? I'll dry.'

Too stunned to protest, she gave it to him.

'Strange,' he ruminated, as she washed the last item and then quickly wiped down the tiled worktops, 'I'd never have envisaged you as the housewifely type.'

'Why, because I'm having an affair with a married man?'

She regretted the goad the moment it left her lips. Why on earth did she always fall into the trap of letting her impulsive tongue overrule caution? She saw from his frown that she had angered him. They were going to be cooped up in his car for heaven alone knew how long, and she had had to go and destroy his earlier fairly benign mood by reminding him of David!

'May I use your bathroom?'

The request caught her off guard, and then she nodded her head and directed him to it.

The flat only had one bedroom and the bathroom was off it. She had decorated them when she had first moved, incorporating the soft pink-peach sanitaryware into a colour scheme that was wholly feminine.

The single bed she had had ever since she was a teenager had come to London with her, and on the chair beside her bed was the now rather tatty teddy bear that her parents had given to her for her first birthday.

Her jacket was already in the hall, money, a notebook, tape recorder and everything else she would need in the capacious leather bag she always carried with her.

When Hazard rejoined her, he looked oddly withdrawn and engrossed in his own thoughts.

His Jaguar had only two proper seats, and Susannah, who had decided that she would opt for sitting in the back, away from him, grimaced faintly. She was just reaching for the door-handle when Hazard forestalled her, opening it for her, his fingers just brushing hers as she did so. A tingle of electric sensation rushed through her, freezing her where she stood.

'Strange sort of lover you have,' he remarked caustically. 'Doesn't buy you a double bed, doesn't open car doors for you . . .'

Bending low to get into the car, Susannah was relieved that he couldn't see her face. She had forgotten about her small single bed; far too small for two people to share in comfort.

'But, of course, I'm forgetting. He doesn't sleep over, does he?' Hazard taunted her, settling himself beside her in the driver's seat. 'Don't you ever want a man you could really call your own, Susannah, instead of having to share him with someone else—someone who has far more right to him than you? Don't you have any guilt about what you're doing? Don't you . . .'

'It's over . . . I'm not seeing him any more.'

Susannah wasn't sure which of them was the more shocked. Hazard, who had just been about to fire the engine, stiffened and then turned towards her.

'Run that by me again,' he demanded tensely.

'It's over. The affair . . .'

Her voice shook, the tension in the air between them making her so physically aware of him that it was frightening.

'It's over?'

It was as though he couldn't take in what she was saying, and no wonder. What on earth had made her blurt it out like that? It came to her as they looked at one another that they themselves might have been two lovers, rather than adversaries. The thought heated her skin, pinpricks of awareness tormenting her nerve-endings. Against her will, she remembered the night of the party, the way Hazard had touched and kissed her.

'When?' The hoarse demand shocked her back to reality.

Too late, she remembered why she had been so determined not to tell Hazard the truth.

The sexuality which had so intimidated her had never been more in evidence. She shrank from it instinctively, both attracted and repelled by it. She wasn't used to such intensely sexual men. David had not been like that, and before him her relationships had never run very deep. Casual dates, male friends whom she had never allowed to penetrate the citadel of her private self, either emotionally or physically.

'Why didn't you tell me before?'

Almost too late, she sprang to her own defence, her manner cool and distant, as she responded acidly, 'Perhaps because I didn't consider it was any of your business. You're my boss, Hazard, not my keeper.'

She sat back in her seat, deliberately closing her eyes, trying to enforce her determination not to allow him to pursue the conversation.

Even with her eyes closed, she was intensely aware of him, more aware in some senses: she could feel the heat emanating from his body, smell its personal male scent. He started the car, and his arm accidentally brushed against her thigh as he changed gear. Instantly, rivulets of sensations burned through her veins.

'Susannah.'

The sound of her name, spoken for once with gentleness, instead of the harshness to which she had grown accustomed, made her open her eyes. His were warm and far more friendly than she had ever seen them before.

'Why don't we start again, wipe the past off the slate? Start afresh.'

Some deep feminine instinct for self-preservation warned her not to accept. This man spelled danger for her; she knew it just as she knew that no one else had ever had the power to make her react physically to him in the way that he could. At the moment, that knowledge was hers and hers alone. Once she dropped her defences, though... She shivered slightly, and instantly he was concerned.

'Cold? I'll put the heater on.'

Just for a moment, she allowed herself to imagine what it would be like to be wrapped in his concern twenty-four hours a day, what it would be like to bask in his approval full time. And then, determinedly, she thrust the thought away from her and forced a calm smile to her lips.

'Well?' he asked her softly. 'Do we have a bargain? A new, clean start?'

What could she say? To refuse would be both churlish and dangerous.

She nodded, unable to speak for the sudden lump of emotion in her throat. She had reached a momentous point in her life, a point of almost mystic importance; she sensed it and yet at the same time she wanted to deny it.

'Was that nod a yes?'

She wasn't sure how to react to him in this light-hearted, almost teasing, mood.

'Yes.'

'Good.'

Surely he was closer to her than he had been before? The grey eyes mesmerised her as they came closer. The car had stopped, and she gave a soft gasp as his hands left the wheel and he gathered her closer. His hands felt warm through the thinness of her shirt, and Susannah shivered beneath their slow caress.

'No. Please don't . . .'

She wasn't sure what she was pleading for him not to do. Her brain felt like cotton wool, her will-power a practically non-existent thing that refused any aid.

His head bent and she quivered beneath the light brush of his lips against her own.

Like the magnificence of the sun suddenly illuminating the earth at dawn, she realised why it was she had fought so hard to keep him at arm's length. She was in love with him!

She closed her eyes in shock, trying to pull away, but Hazard's arms only tightened, his mouth hardening over hers. A thrill of pleasure ran through her, her lips softening and clinging. He made a sound deep in his throat; a deep male sound of appreciation of her acceptance of him, and she was lost, her whole body quivering with repressed yearning.

Here was the man who could arouse her as David had never done, who touched the innermost core of her both emotionally and physically.

'I wanted you the first moment I set eyes on you, do you know that?'

Susannah caught the thick, muffled words as he mouthed them against her lips, and her senses quickened to a state of bemused delight. His hand found her breast and the pleasure grew. She heard a soft female moan of acquiescence and realised with shock that it was her own. She felt like someone who had stepped out of reality into another dimension. His tongue touched her lips, tracing their soft moistness, and she quivered with mute pleasure.

'God, you don't know what you do to me! You've put me through hell these last weeks, do you know that?'

Hell because he wanted her, or hell because he thought she was involved with a married man? Susannah was in no state to ask.

Was this really what she had feared when she had pretended that she was still involved with David, when she had lied and told him that she had simply been using him as a substitute for her non-existent lover?

It seemed incredible, in her sensually dazed state, that she had ever feared this bliss. It was what she had been born for; it was the culmination of all she had ever wanted out of life.

As he felt the quivering response pulse through her, Hazard groaned, trying to manoeuvre them both so that they could be closer together.

'I think you must be a secret masochist,' he muttered against her hair. 'Of all the places to choose to tell me . . . I can't make love to you here. If it wasn't for the fact that we're due to interview your author . . .'

Make love to her? She trembled violently beneath the onslaught of physical response his words invoked, and he felt it run through her body and cursed.

'Yes. Yes, I know, and I want you too, but not here...' He lifted his head and looked into her eyes, and Susannah's heart jumped at the glazed ache of desire she saw in his. 'Feel what you're doing to me.'

His hand covered hers, placing it against his flesh. Hot colour scalded her skin and he laughed.

'Shy? I can hardly believe it.'

His words brought her back to reality. He thought she was a sexually experienced and available woman, while in reality...

'At this moment, there's nothing I want more than to take you to bed, but I'm afraid right now that's impossible. Have dinner with me tonight?'

He took her silence for assent, and no wonder, after the way she had just behaved, she berated herself, retiring to her own side of the car and running her fingers through her tousled hair as he set the car in motion.

Hazard swore suddenly, braking hard, and she froze, half expecting to see they were about to hit something. When she looked at him, there was a white line of tension around his mouth and his eyes were glittering with the intensity of his emotions.

'What is it? What's wrong?'

He was looking at her, and suddenly she realised why. The movement of her arms as she tried to restore some sort of order to her hair had dragged the fine material of her shirt taut across her breasts, outlining both their shape and the hard arousal of her nipples.

They were still in the car park, and with one swift movement he bent his head, pulling her towards him so that she was turned into the curve of his body. His hand cupped her breast, his thumb stroking urgently across her nipple, and then to her shock she felt the moist heat of his mouth possessing her aroused flesh. Even through the fabric of her shirt and bra she could feel the heat of his mouth. Her body ached and pulsed with fierce need, her hands going up to hold his head, her fingers pushing urgently through the thick darkness of his hair.

The sound of a car horn out on the street brought them both back to reality. Hazard released her reluctantly, breathing hard as he sat back in his seat. Tiny beads of perspiration dampened his skin, and the aroused, musky male scent of him filled the car. Once, she would have found him frightening, now...now she found it arousing, she admitted shakily, fighting for her own self-control.

'Come on,' Hazard said hoarsely. 'Let's get out of here. The sooner we get this interview out of the way, the sooner we can be alone.'

After that, it was impossible for the day not to be a success. They were lucky with the traffic and found the motorway relatively unclogged with cars.

Hazard was a confident and competent driver with whom she felt completely at ease. They stopped once, just off the motorway, for coffee and something to eat, but neither of them were disposed to linger.

In an effort to restore some sort of normality to events, Susannah told him all she knew about Emma King. He tried to draw her out about her own life, but she was reluctant to tell him too much, in case he guessed how much she had been deceiving him.

He would have to know some time; she accepted that. They were going to become lovers, that was inevitable, but she could face the problem when it arose. She was an active young woman of twenty-four, her virginity might be no more than a technicality, rather than a physical barrier. She wasn't going to start worrying now about his reaction to the truth; she wanted to enjoy what she was experiencing without any worries to mar it.

During the drive, the weather had gradually worsened, but inside the protection of the warm car it was possible to ignore the sheeting rain and howling winds. However, once they neared York, and Hazard switched on the car radio, they began to learn how grim the weather conditions actually were. The Ouse had risen rapidly, and parts of York were apparently in danger of flooding.

Frowning slightly as he concentrated on the news bulletin, Hazard turned up the radio. He had good hands, Susannah noticed, her body melting on a surge of awareness of him: long and lean, with clean blunt nails.

Now that she was prepared to admit herself that at the root of her fear of and antagonism towards him lay a much more potent and far different emotion, it was as though a door had opened in her life, allowing her to step through into a new world.

With David, she had never been free to give full rein to her emotions, they had always been something she had had to guard cautiously and fearfully; but, amazingly, especially after her experience with David, with Hazard she felt an immediate and intense trust. It was like coming into a room that was heated with a warm fire, after being out in the cold.

Perhaps once, before her parents' deaths, she had experienced the same feeling, but never since. Oh, Aunt Emily had been a marvellous substitute parent, but she had brought Susannah up on the same diet of stern remoteness which had guided her own youth. Odd how, until she was actually experiencing it, she had not realised quite what she had missed.

'You're quiet. Something wrong?'

A quick look into Hazard's face showed the genuine depth of his concern. She shook her head.

'I think I'm still rather overwhelmed by the speed of . . . things.'

'Yes, I've had a little more time to get used to the idea, I suppose,' he agreed. 'I know what you mean, though. Before I met you, I had no idea . . .' He broke off and Susannah was surprised to see a faint dull flush of colour stain his skin. For a moment, he had almost looked . . . guilty! She had seen the expression so often in David's eyes, she was hardly likely to mistake it.

'Could you check the directions for me? I think we're on the right road.'

It was probably just that, like her, Hazard was rather overwhelmed by the turn of events, Susannah comforted herself as she picked up the map.

Emma King lived in an isolated farmhouse in a remote part of the flat plain surrounding York and, as Hazard drove, Susannah kept getting glimpses of the ominously swollen Ouse.

'We're looking for a sign for Bywater,' Hazard told her, momentarily slowing down, his hand brushing hers as he looked down at the map.

If the merest touch of his hand could send her weak with delight, what was she going to feel like when . . .

'No, I think we're still on the right road. It's only a couple of miles on, though. Are you sure you're all right?' He looked at her with such concern that she practically melted with pleasure.

'Yes. Yes, I'm fine.'

Now it was her turn to colour, the intimacy of her thoughts turning her pale skin pink.

What would it be like to cradle Hazard's body in her arms, to run her fingers over his skin? Was he tanned all over? A tiny shudder of sensation began deep inside her and spread quickly through her body.

'Susannah?'

She turned blindly to look at him as she caught the note of worry in Hazard's voice.

'Don't . . . For God's sake, don't look at me like that!'

The raw male growl thickening his voice made her pulses race with excitement. Never in her whole life had she been so aware of her vulnerability.

'I want you,' he groaned thickly. 'I want to take you in my arms and make love to you, and I know that you want it, too.'

'Yes.'

The whispered admission darkened Hazard's eyes, his hands clenching on the steering wheel.

'You choose the damnedest times, you know that, don't you?'

She could only look helplessly at him.

'There's the signpost.' Her voice shook breathlessly.

Hazard cursed as he almost missed the turning, and the tide of desire rising up inside her retreated as Susannah forced herself to concentrate on their surroundings.

They passed through the small village Emma King had described. The river was already lapping over its banks, and Susannah was not surprised to see a small group of people watching it with concern.

Emma King's home was six miles outside the village; a sizeable stone-built rambling building set among what, on a fine day, was no doubt beautiful countryside, but which at the moment was obscured from view by the curtain of heavy rain.

A white-painted farm gate stood open, and Hazard drove through it and parked.

As Susannah made to get out of the car, Hazard forestalled her. 'You wait there until she opens the door. You'll get soaked.'

He was right, she admitted, watching him dash across to the front door and knock.

Seconds passed and Hazard knocked again. Susannah glanced at her watch worriedly. They were virtually on time, only a few minutes late, quite a feat after such a journey, and she did not think Emma was the sort of woman who made appointments and then forgot all about them.

'I'll go and have a look round the back,' Hazard called out to her. 'These old farmhouses have thick walls. There might be a bell round there.'

He was back within minutes.

'We've got a problem,' he told Susannah abruptly. 'She's had a fall. I can't tell how bad it is without

moving her, and I can't do that. Apparently she came
out to check on the river—it runs a hundred yards or
so from the back of the house—and slipped on the
cobbles. Will you stay with her, while I drive down
to the village for the doctor? It will be quicker than
trying to raise him on the phone.'

'Yes, yes, of course.' Concern quickened
Susannah's footsteps as she followed him round the
back of the house, and it deepened when she saw the
writer lying on the wet cobbles.

'There's a rug in the boot of the car,' Hazard told
her. 'I'll go and get it. She's soaked through already,
but . . .'

'There's no need to talk about me as though I'm
not here, you know.'

Relief spread through Susannah as the older woman
spoke.

'Don't try to move,' she warned her, as Emma
struggled to sit up. 'Hazard is going to go for the
doctor.'

'I think it's only a sprain.' She tried to move and
winced. 'Stupid of me to come out in these wretched
high heels instead of wearing boots, but the weather
forecast warned that the Ouse was rising rapidly, and
I wanted to check.'

'You're too far away to suffer flooding, surely?'
Susannah asked her.

'Here, yes, but not in the village. We've had several
floods down there and, when something like this
happens, it's a case of all hands on deck.' She winced
as, inadvertently, she moved and jarred her twisted
ankle.

Hazard produced the rug, and draped it carefully over her. 'I'll be as quick as I can,' he promised.

'A very capable and charming man,' Emma pronounced as Hazard drove off.

'He's my boss.' Susannah avoided Emma's eyes, her emotions too new to share with anyone else.

There was nothing she could do to make Emma more comfortable, so instead she tried to distract her by talking to her. At the very least, there must be a danger to her from exposure, Susannah reflected, shivering herself as the rain beat down on them. Emma wasn't a young woman, and even a short time lying out here, exposed to such weather...

'Don't worry. I'm pretty tough.'

Emma must have read her mind, Susannah thought, starting a little, but the sound of a car drew her attention, easing her anxiety.

'Here's Hazard,' she announced with relief.

'And Dr Barnes... That's her car coming down the lane, I think. She said when I saw her last week that it needed a new exhaust.'

In no time at all, the doctor and Hazard had Emma safely installed in her bedroom. Left to her own devices downstairs, Susannah noticed that the old-fashioned boiler needed stoking. She remembered that Emma had told her that, as yet, their remote village did not have access to gas, and it was a simple enough task to go outside and find the outhouse containing the fuel. It took her back to her childhood, and Aunt Emily's temperamental Aga, which had to be fed with solid fuel at regular intervals.

She made a pot of tea, quickly familiarising herself with the foibles of the old-fashioned range. It was very similar to Aunt Emily's Aga, and soon responded to Susannah's deft coaxing.

Dr Barnes was a tall, slim woman in her mid-thirties, who looked rather tired and drawn.

'My goodness, how on earth did you manage that?' she asked, looking impressed when Susannah proffered the tea. 'That range is a monster. I've told Emma that she ought to get rid of it and either go on to electricity or bottled Gaz, but she won't.' She frowned, and pushed a tired hand into her hair. 'Her ankle's only sprained, but really I should take her into hospital for observation. However, she's a stubborn lady and flatly refuses, and if I'm honest I would have the devil of a job getting her into a bed. She can't stay here on her own, though; she has a niece who lives in York who would come and look after her, but apparently she's away with her husband at the moment, out of the country, and not expected back until tomorrow afternoon.'

'I could stay.'

The words were out before Susannah realised what she was saying. Guiltily, she looked across at Hazard. He was, after all, her boss, and he might not take too kindly to the idea of her volunteering her services.

'I've got a better idea,' he said calmly. 'We'll both stay.'

'Well, if you could...' Dr Barnes looked relieved. 'Conditions are rather primitive here, I'm afraid. There *is* electricity, but we've been warned to expect high winds tonight, and that will probably cause disruptions in the service. Emma does have some oil lamps. What am I doing, putting you off?' she asked wryly. 'If you *don't* stay, I'm going to have to conjure up a nurse from somewhere, and heaven alone knows how I'm going to do that.'

'We're staying,' Hazard told her firmly. 'We wouldn't dream of leaving Emma alone.'

'She's lucky to have such good friends.' The doctor stood up, giving Hazard a warm smile, before Susannah could point out that he hadn't even met the older woman before today.

She was jealous, she recognised, suddenly realising why she was experiencing such sharp pangs of resentment over that exchanged smile. And it was ridiculous.

'I'd better go. I've got several more calls to make. Thanks for the tea.' She smiled at Susannah, but not as warmly as she had smiled at Hazard. 'Good luck with the boiler.'

'I'd better go up and tell Emma that we're staying,' Susannah said awkwardly once they were alone. She was suddenly experiencing a sensation of feeling almost tongue-tied and oddly shy.

'I'll come with you, just in case she turns awkward,' Hazard told her with a grin.

As he opened the kitchen door for her, he caught hold of her arm and said softly, 'You know, you're one hell of a lady, Susannah. Not a bit as I'd imagined you to be. Generous, warm-hearted—all the things a woman should be.'

'I'm glad you approve.'

She had meant to sound cool and mocking, but instead her voice wobbled slightly, and her breathing became suspended as Hazard bent his head and whispered against her mouth, 'Oh, I approve.'

He kissed her slowly and thoroughly, his mouth firm and warm against her own. It was like sinking into a warm bath, Susannah thought mistily as she responded to the seduction of his kiss.

He released her reluctantly, pushing her gently towards the door.

'There you are, the Hazard Maine seal of approval.'

The look in his eyes told her much more than the words. If only they were completely alone, she could show him just . . . but they weren't, and Emma was no doubt lying upstairs, worrying about what was going to happen. The habit of responsibility instilled in her by Aunt Emily was too strong to ignore. Resolutely Susannah turned away from Hazard and headed for the stairs.

CHAPTER SIX

DESPITE her objections, Susannah sensed Emma's relief when she was told of their plans.

The cupboards and freezer were well stocked, she told her, so they need have no worries about running out of food.

'Whether or not you'll be able to eat anything hot, though, is another matter. The range...'

'I think I can handle it,' Susannah told her, explaining that she had virtually grown up with something very similar.

'There's a chicken in the fridge that I was going to cook for lunch. Perhaps we could have that tonight...'

'A good idea,' Susannah agreed. 'Is there anything you'd like? Something to read?'

In point of fact, Dr Barnes had told them that she had given Emma a sedative that would make her sleep but, guessing that the older woman would try to fight its effects if she knew, Susannah said nothing.

'No, I don't think so, thank you, my dear. To be honest, I'm feeling rather tired.'

'I won't disturb you, then.'

'Please make yourselves at home. I'm afraid I can't provide Hazard with anything in the way of pyjamas—my husband never wore them. You'll find aired sheets and pillowslips in the airing cupboard, and there's a nightdress in the bottom drawer in the chest in the next bedroom. One of my nieces bought it for me, but it isn't my style.' She chuckled. 'To be honest, I prefer a pair of thermal pyjamas these days; I always get so terribly cold in bed. My late husband used to complain that my feet felt like blocks of ice.' She sighed and yawned, and Susannah suspected that, by the time she was downstairs, Emma would be fast asleep.

'There's a phone in Emma's study,' Hazard told her when she got downstairs. 'We don't need to alert the office at this stage, but if you've made any arrangements for the weekend...'

'None,' Susannah told him. 'You...you don't have to stay on,' she added, hoping her voice would not give away how much she wanted him to. 'I...I think I can manage.'

'I'm staying. Think what they're going to say to us at work when we get back?' he teased her. 'The pair of us, virtually alone here, in a remote farmhouse!'

Reporters had fertile minds, and Susannah pressed her hands to her hot face as she contemplated the type of remarks her colleagues were likely to make.

'Don't look so anguished. No one need know.'

Why did she feel he had withdrawn from her slightly? She looked at him and saw that his eyes were faintly shadowed.

'I'm sorry. It's just that I'm not used...' She broke off, uncomfortably aware of where her unguarded words were leading her, and her flush deepened. Her guilt at deceiving him, not once but twice, brought a small worried frown to her forehead.

'You know, you amaze me at times! One minute the hardened sophisticate, the next, a shy innocent...'

Desperate to stop him probing, Susannah forced a brittle laugh. 'That's women for you. All of us a part-chameleon!'

'I think I'd better take a look at the boiler.' Hazard started moving away from her.

'It's all right for the moment. I stoked it while you were upstairs with the doctor. Which reminds me, I'd better do something about that chicken.' She turned towards the fridge.

'I'll go outside and take a look at the river. Dr Barnes warned me that they're expecting severe flooding in the village. If that happens, we'll be marooned up here, because that's the only road out.' She didn't turn round as Hazard opened the back door. It felt odd being alone here with him—odd and exciting! It was extraordinary how easily she had been able to overcome her initial hostility to him.

The chicken was a plump, large one, and Emma's cupboards proved to be as well stocked as she had promised. A cold, stone pantry yielded enough apples for a pie, and she was just coring and slicing the fruit when Hazard came back in.

'It isn't looking good,' he told her. 'If this rain doesn't let up in the next half an hour or so, I think we're definitely going to be cut off.'

'Well, we won't starve. Emma has enough food in for a siege. Oh no, you don't!' She rapped Hazard briefly over the knuckles as he pinched a piece of apple. 'Those are for my pie.'

'Mmm . . . And what are these for?'

She had found some plump raisins which would add a slightly more spicy touch to her pie.

'They're for the pie as well, so hands off,' she told him succinctly. 'I'll go up and check on Emma once I've finished here.'

'Mm...' Hazard filched another slice of apple, munching it with relish. 'I suppose we ought to give some thought to where we're going to sleep, and when. Dr Barnes mentioned that there might be a possibility of Emma suffering from exposure, which suggests that one of us ought to be with her all night.'

'We'll have to take it in turns. When I go up to see her, I'll make up our beds. There should be time before our meal's ready.'

She didn't look at Hazard as she spoke, but her hands shook betrayingly.

'Hey.' Slowly, he turned her round to face him, ignoring her protests about her floury hands. 'Is that really what you think of me? That I'm crass enough to expect you spend tonight with me? Maybe in different circumstances, if we'd both had enough time together first to relax; and only then if it was a mutual decision. I'm not going to pretend that I don't want you, Susannah. You know better than that. But the first time we go to bed together I want it to be something special, not something rushed and furtive.'

His words were so sincere, his expression so ruefully tender, that she didn't even try to resist the impulse to put her head on his shoulder.

'You must think me such a fool.'

'For not rushing into bed with me? No, Susannah. I'd be more inclined to think you a fool if you did. Let's get one thing clear. I've had my moments; I'm no saint, I'm afraid, but I'm not promiscuous, either. No one with any degree of self-worth can afford to be these days. Now isn't our time, but it will come, I promise you that.'

Gently he kissed her, his hands cupping Susannah's face, his lips teasing hers until a small sound of frustration made his hold on her tighten and his mouth claim hers in fierce male responsiveness.

All the things she couldn't tell him in words—her trust, her love, her inexperience—she tried to communicate to him in that kiss. When he eventually set her free, she was flushed, her eyes brilliant with arousal. What price now caution or lack of experience? If he were to pick her up in his arms and . . .

'Don't! Don't look at me like that,' he groaned, catching hold of her wrist and lifting her hand, palm upwards, to his mouth.

The sensation of his lips moving against her tender skin, his teeth nibbling the base of her fingers, made her weak with desire.

'I must go and see Emma.'

Reluctantly, she stepped back from him as he let her go.

'Yes. I think you must,' he responded gravely. 'Don't trust too much to my self-control, Susannah,' he warned her as she headed for the stairs. 'It's been one hell of a long time since I've wanted a woman the way I want you.'

Her heart was pounding by the time she got upstairs, whether from his words or from the exertion she wasn't sure, but she suspected the former.

Emma was deeply asleep. Closing her door gently, Susannah investigated the other bedrooms. There were three of them, all of them large and all with comfortable-looking double beds.

She decided she would have the one closest to Emma's room. Hazard had driven them all the way up here; he was bound to be tired later, and Susannah was determined that *she* was the one who would sit with Emma during the night. If she had the room next to her, it would be that little bit easier to convince Hazard that she was right.

She made up both the bed in that room, and that in the room next to the bathroom.

She found the nightdress Emma had offered her, and smoothed out the soft cotton with amazed fingers. It was Victorian, the cotton soft and smooth, its yoke and cuffs lavishly adorned with lace.

Had some long-ago Victorian girl dreamed of the man to whom she would give her love as she sewed this nightgown? Telling herself this was no time to start day-dreaming, Susannah sighed and placed it reverently on her bed.

She was half-way downstairs when the lights started to flicker. She had put them on because the overcast sky had made the afternoon dark.

'I think this is where Dr Barnes's prophecy concerning the power cut comes true,' Hazard called up to her.

'I suspect you may be right.'

'So where do we find the oil lamps, I wonder?'

'They're in an outbuilding next to the fuel store. I saw them when I was looking for the fuel.'

'Right, and I'll go out and get them, and bring them in.'

'I think that might be a good idea,' Susannah agreed as the lights flickered wildly.

Emma's range seemed a good deal less temperamental than her aunt's Aga. As she checked on the chicken and her pie, Susannah found herself wondering what sort of bread it made, her mouth watering tormentingly. The last time she had eaten had been at breakfast. She had only had coffee on the way, since the original idea had been that they would have lunch with Emma. Lunch was more likely to be served at a time favoured by Yorkshire folk for high tea.

'This takes me back to my summer camp days,' Hazard announced walking in with the lamps and some fuel.

'Summer camp?' Susannah queried.

'An American institution,' he told her with a grin. 'Invented to spare parents the necessity of entertaining their offspring during the long summer holidays. In point of fact it's an excellent idea, and allows the kids to let off steam and learn independence at the same time.'

'You're American, but you don't have much of an accent.'

'Wrong. I'm British, but my parents emigrated to Australia when I was about seven.'

'Australia?'

'Mmm. Later, my parents were divorced and I went with my mother to America.'

'Does she still live there?'

Almost instantly, she was aware of having trodden on forbidden territory. His hands stilled, his whole stance tense and defensive. 'Yes,' he told her harshly, turning away from her. 'I think we're going to need some matches to get these things lit. Have you seen any?'

Obviously the subject of his mother was not one she was going to be allowed to pursue, Susannah realised, taking the hint, but still hurt by it.

She remembered what Claire had said about him virtually being brought up by Mac, and wondered how true it was. He would have been younger than Caroline by several years, of course. Strange that Richard had said nothing about their relationship when he had announced that Hazard was to take over from him, but perhaps he had felt that Hazard himself might not want details of his personal life bruited around the office. He was obviously very sensitive about it.

'There are some matches over there.' She was determined not to let him see how much his withdrawal had hurt her.

'Well, at least we know they work,' Hazard announced when he had tested the lamps to his satisfaction. 'How long before we eat? I'm beginning to feel very empty.'

Taking her cue from him, Susannah responded equally lightly. It was pointless letting him see how hurt she had been by the barrier he had thrown up. Later, perhaps, when they knew one another better, he might feel more able to confide in her. Men were notorious for not liking to talk about their innermost feelings.

'We'd better organise something for tonight. One of us will have to stay with Emma...'

'It's all taken care of. I'm sleeping in the room next to hers, and I'll spend the night with her. There's a very comfortable chair in her room, and I'm only a light sleeper.' She saw that he was about to argue with her and said quickly, 'Hazard, you drove us here.

Please let me do my bit... It won't be the first time I've done a nursing stint. My aunt broke her arm several years ago, and there were complications.'

'Several years ago? You must have been very young. Didn't your parents...?'

He stopped and she said quietly, 'My parents were killed when I was very young—before my first birthday, in fact. Aunt Emily brought me up. She's really my father's aunt, very strict and a stickler for duty and doing the right thing, but she's also very kind and generous. If it hadn't been for her, I expect I'd have grown up in a foster home, or worse still in an institution. Not that I'm suggesting they aren't excellent at what they do, but there's no substitute for the sort of love and care Aunt Emily gave me.'

'Yes. I know what you mean.'

For a second she thought he was about to go on, but then he got up and moved restlessly around the large kitchen.

'What happened to you, Susannah? From the sort of background you describe, I should have thought you'd be the type of girl who would marry young and spend her life caring for her family. Did you rebel against your aunt's authority? Was that how you ended up with a married lover?'

All of a sudden his voice was harsh, the antagonism back as they stared at one another, and then Susannah said evenly. 'No. That had nothing to do with Aunt Emily—or rebellion. And you're wrong. Aunt Emily might have taught me all the old-fashioned domestic skills, but she taught me them for my own benefit, not so that I would become someone's wife. Before she retired, Aunt Emily was a li-

brarian. She encouraged me to do well at school and
have my own career. In fact, in many ways, I suspect
she's something of a feminist.' A small reminiscent
smile curled her mouth. 'She certainly doesn't subscribe to the view that man is superior to woman...far
from it.'

She was trying to recapture their previous light-
hearted mood. She didn't want to talk about David,
nor to have to explain. To explain meant going into
things she still felt too insecure to discuss. Like the
fact that she never felt totally at ease with her
peers...like the fact that David, being older and less
aggressively sexual, had put her at her ease, made her
feel comfortable and unthreatened. She couldn't tell
Hazard yet how naïve she had been; how she had never
even guessed that David was married. If she did, he
might guess at her total lack of knowledge of his sex,
and with that knowledge might come the realisation
of how inexperienced she was. Sexually inhibited, so
she had been told. Was it true? Certainly once she
might have accepted that it was, but now...knowing
how she felt the moment Hazard touched her, she was
beginning to wonder. He made her experience an intensity of need she hadn't known could exist.

'You're offended, and rightly so. I shouldn't have
brought up the subject of your affair. Is it really over,
Susannah?'

Her heart overflowed with love and humility as she
caught the uncertainty in his voice. He hadn't been
sitting in moral judgement, he had simply been
jealous.

'Yes,' she told him simply and honestly. 'And it...'

And it wasn't even really an affair, she had been about to admit, driven to make a clean breast of her deception by a growing need to feel that there were no barriers between them.

'No,' Hazard interrupted her harshly. 'Don't tell me any more. I'm starving. How long before we eat?'

Accepting his cue, Susannah walked across to the range and investigated its contents.

'Whenever you're ready. I'd better go and check on Emma, though.'

'My turn.' She couldn't escape from the feeling that he wanted to put some distance between them—and it hurt, no matter how much she tried to be logical and calm.

He was gone for about five minutes and, as Susannah had already guessed before he returned, he announced that Emma was now awake.

'She's still very dopey, though. She says we're to make ourselves completely at home, and apologised for causing us any trouble. She doesn't want anything to eat just yet.'

'I'd thought of making some soup from the chicken carcass. If I cut off all the flesh tonight, I could make the soup for her supper.'

'Home-made soup?' His eyebrows lifted.

'Aunt Emily abhorred waste,' Susannah told him, mock primly.

'Mmm ... I think I'm going to want to meet Aunt Emily, if only to see that she exists and that you're not sending me up.'

'Oh, she exists,' Susannah told him wryly. 'And, if you do meet her, she'll bombard you with a hundred questions about what you do and who your parents

were.' She grimaced faintly, remembering the tongue-
tied silence to which her formidable aunt had reduced
her first adolescent boyfriends.

She had never taken David home. Once she'd realised he was married she hadn't been able to, knowing
how her aunt would have felt about their relationship.

The kitchen was the old farmhouse type with a large
scrubbed table. Hazard found cutlery in one of its
drawers, while Susannah put the finishing touches to
the sauce she had made for the chicken.

'I won't ask you to carve it,' she told him when she
lifted it out of the range. She had cooked it in the
way Aunt Emily had taught her years ago; its flesh
looked moist and succulent, ready to fall off the
bones.

'Roast potatoes? Marvellous,' Hazard approved
hungrily.

'I'm afraid it won't be anything like what you're
used to eating.' She remembered how she had seen
him dining at the Connaught and quailed a little.

'No, it won't,' he agreed wryly. 'You don't know
how tired I am of restaurant meals. This will be a real
treat for me.'

Susannah drained the vegetables, and placed them
on the serving dish with the chicken and potatoes.
Putting it on the table, she deftly transferred the sauce
into the waiting boat.

'If you enjoy the pleasures of home cooking so
much, I'm surprised you haven't married,' she remarked as she sat at the table. She was fishing and
she knew it, but she was curious to know how a man
of his age and eligibility had managed to remain single
so long.

Hazard passed her the serving dish, replying seriously, 'After my parents' divorce, I swore I'd never get married unless I was sure it was going to last.'

Yes, she could understand that the sundering of his parents' marriage could have that effect on an intelligent pre-adolescent.

'What about you? Or are you a committed career woman?'

'I enjoy my career, yes. But these days it's perfectly possible for a woman to have both a career and a husband and family.'

'You want children?'

Susannah paused for a moment. 'Yes, I think so.'

I want your children, she wanted to say, and the intensity with which that need gripped her made her insides tremble and ache.

'And you?'

'There's a certain primitive part of me that says yes; a basic male desire to fulfil the role nature fitted me for. Yes. But modern war, seen at close hand, makes one fearful of what the future might hold for all children. In Beirut, they know more about bombs and guns than they do about fairy-tales and Father Christmas.'

Did that mean he did or did not want a family? Susannah still wasn't quite sure.

'You are a wonderful cook,' he complimented her, pushing away his empty plate. 'One day, you must let *me* cook a meal for *you*, although I doubt I could cook anything on that monster.'

'Oh, it's quite friendly, really. Would you like some pie?'

'Please.'

There was a certain dangerous appeal in watching a hungry man devour food you'd prepared especially for him, Susannah reflected wryly. Mother Nature was clever and cunning in her determination to have her own way!

'Now it's your turn to sit down,' Hazard told her when he had finished. 'I'll make us both some coffee, and then I'll do the washing up.'

He had just returned to the table when the lights flickered and then abruptly went out.

'I think we just lost the electricity. Pity, I was looking forward to a nice hot shower tonight.'

'You can still have that. The boiler heats the water,' Susannah told him, adding teasingly, 'You really are a city boy, aren't you? No electricity, and you think the world's come to an end.'

'Not really. There were times when Ma and I had it pretty rough after Dad left. We were living in Sydney at the time, in a rented house. Ma didn't work, she never had and couldn't really. There was no way she could pay the rent, so we had to move out and into rooms.' His face grew shadowed and Susannah could see that his memories weren't happy ones.

'What did you do?' she encouraged softly, sensing that he wanted to talk, and yet that he was at the same time reluctant to do so.

'I got a job delivering newspapers, only I cut out the middle man.' His face grew shuttered. 'I'd better go and light those lamps. It's getting dark.'

It was, and it was still raining, Susannah realised when she got up to go and look through the window.

'We could light a fire in the sitting-room, if you like,' she suggested. 'There are some books in there, and Emma did tell us to make ourselves at home.'

'No, we might as well stay in here, unless you . . .'

Susannah shook her head. She liked the homely, comfortable kitchen.

They washed up together in a companionable silence and, while Susannah started to make the chicken soup, Hazard went out to get more fuel for the boiler.

When he came back, he was soaked.

'The wind,' he told her. 'It's practically blowing a gale out there!'

'I'll go upstairs and get you a towel,' Susannah offered, but Hazard shook his head.

'I've got a better idea. Why don't I go up and have that shower now?'

'Fine. By the time you come back, this should be finished, then I can take a tray up to Emma.'

'What a pity we don't know one another better,' he teased as he turned towards the stairs. 'Then I could have asked you to join me.'

Laughing at her pink cheeks, he went upstairs.

Share a shower with him! Susannah's stomach muscles contracted, a hot, sweet lethargy sweeping over her. If she closed her eyes, she could almost picture his naked body, almost feel the satin dampness of his skin, almost taste the male freshness of it . . .

She shuddered, opening her eyes, shocked by the sensuality of her thoughts. She had just lifted the soup from the hotplate when she heard him call her name.

As she rushed to the bottom of the stairs, Hazard was standing at the top looking down at her, naked apart from the very brief towel he had wrapped around his hips.

For an aeon of time, she could do nothing other than stare at him, hungrily absorbing the male perfection of him, as though every one of her senses had fasted on purpose for this moment.

Rivulets of moisture ran down his bare chest, glinting under the lamplight in the sleek darkness of his body hair.

'Bath towels,' he asked her huskily. 'I can't seem to find them.'

Towels! Of course, she had forgotten to tell him they were in the airing cupboard and that was in her room. Thoroughly flustered, she hurried into it.

'They're here.'

She only realised he had followed her when she saw him standing in the doorway, holding up the lantern he was carrying.

'Here you are.'

She put the towels down on her bed, not trusting herself to so much as touch him. She had never known there could be a physical wanting like this. It shocked her. It excited her too, she acknowledged, turning her burning face away from him.

'Don't do that.'

He had moved so quietly she hadn't heard him, and she tensed as he turned her round, tilting her face so that he could look down into it.

'Why are you embarrassed? Don't you know what it does to me to see that you want me?'

'I . . .'

The denial which years of Aunt Emily's upbringing told her she should make stuck in her throat.

'You want me,' Hazard repeated. 'I can see it here.' His thumb brushed the corners of her eyes. 'And here.' His hands slid down until they cupped the fullness of her breasts. 'Oh God, Susannah!'

'Emma...' she protested weakly as Hazard put down the lamp and drew her trembling body into his arms.

'Still asleep. I looked in on her earlier. Let me love you, Susannah,' he whispered thickly against her mouth. 'Let me love you the way I've been wanting to from the first time I saw you.'

CHAPTER SEVEN

SUSANNAH could have stopped him. She could have drawn back, but she had no thought of doing either.

The moment Hazard's mouth touched hers, everything else was forgotten. Her lips crushed against his in the heat of his kiss. She was melting, dissolving into a whirlpool of pure pleasure, her mouth opening eagerly at the fierce probe of his tongue. Tiny shudders of pleasure ran through her as his tongue-tip sought the soft moistness of her mouth, and then caressed her tongue itself, coaxing it into making seductive forays of its own.

She felt his shudder as she shyly probed the unknown masculinity of his mouth, and then before she could retreat he was drawing her tongue deeper into captivity, sucking gently on it in a way that made her whole body tremble with arousal, even after the kiss had ended.

'Do it to me,' she heard him saying thickly against her ear. 'Kiss me. Show me that you want me.'

Blindly, she followed his lead, copying the intimate caress, delighting in the way his muscles tensed beneath her hands.

He pulled away, holding her shoulders, staring down into her flushed face, his breathing rapid and uneven.

'I want you, and I want you now. What is it that you do to me? You make me lose control and forget.' He closed his eyes, momentarily hiding their febrile glitter from her, his body arching back slightly to reveal the male line of his throat. He looked like a man caught up in something he could no longer control, and on impulse Susannah pressed her lips against the taut column of his throat, trying to comfort him.

It was the wrong thing to do; she realised it instantly. The salt taste of his skin, its warmth and scent, released emotions inside her that had nothing to do with comfort. Beneath her lips she felt his throat move, and her mouth opened, unable to resist the temptation.

She heard him groan, and her heart beat wildly as she recognised the uncontrollable need in the sound.

Hazard picked her up and she clung to him, wordlessly. He undressed her quickly, but not roughly; sensing his impatience, Susannah struggled to help him, her love for him overwhelming her as he paused for a moment to gently trace the fullness of her breasts.

'Beautiful,' he told her reverently, 'so very beautiful.'

He looked like a pagan god, outlined in the thin light of the lantern: his skin dark, his hair unruly, his classic, sculptured profile thrown into relief. He looked like the kind of lover every woman dreams of having, she admitted, her heart skipping a beat as he knelt beside her, wrenching off the damp towel.

His body was shadowed with dark hair. She wondered if it felt as silky as it looked, and reached out tentatively to touch him.

The heat coming off his skin shocked her. She would have drawn back, but Hazard caught hold of her hand, lifting it to his lips, kissing the palm, and then ... Susannah's heart leapt in her throat as he started sucking her fingers. It was the most erotic sensation she had ever experienced! She made a sound of protest in her throat, her eyes huge and glazed as they stared dazedly into his.

'You like that? You're so responsive, so feminine. I want to taste all of you. Every centimetre of your skin. Touch me, Susannah,' he commanded fiercely, releasing her hand to place it against his breastbone. Feel what you do to me.'

Beneath her hand, his flesh burned with heat. She could feel the fierce thud of his heart, and her own raced frantically in time. She moved her hand and felt the soft scrape of body hair against the delicate pads of her fingers. It arrowed downwards over his flat belly, and she traced its descent, wonderingly, her senses registering the harsh charged change in his breathing as she touched.

She wanted to explore all of him. She wanted ... She shuddered mindlessly as he suddenly caught hold of her, dragging her against his body so that she could feel the strength of his arousal.

'Stop torturing me,' he demanded against her ear. 'I want you to love me, Susannah. Oh God, you don't know how much I want that!'

The last few words were muffled against her throat as he moved his head and started caressing her skin with an open-mouthed hunger that drove the last vestiges of hesitation from her mind.

Her hands found his shoulders and she clung to him, her nails digging into his skin. His mouth moved downwards, its descent tormentingly slow.

His tongue teased the areola of her nipple, while she arched against him in frantic supplication, small feminine noises of frustration clogging her throat.

In the faint light, her skin gleamed pearl white, rose-tipped with the darkness of her nipples. His mouth hovered. With a frantic, wordless plea, Susannah arched higher and then cried out sharply in pleasure as she felt the fierce possession of his mouth against her breast.

The sweep of his hands down over her belly, shaping the line of her thighs, and the knowledge that there could be only one outcome to their lovemaking only aroused her even more. The sensation of his skin beneath her fingertips, the fierce contraction of his muscles, the musky man-scent of him, all these were things that delighted her senses.

As she touched him, Hazard trembled and groaned, closing his eyes, his throat arched. He muttered something she couldn't catch, and then caught hold of her, pushing her down against the bed, his mouth hot and demanding as his tongue thrust fiercely against hers. His body moved against her own, taut and restless with passion. She traced the indentation of his spine, her fingers smoothing the flat plain of his buttocks.

'I want you. I want you . . .' murmured Hazard.

Her body adapted itself to the weight of his, her thighs parting, instinct showing her the way, and then abruptly Hazard tensed.

'What is it?' she whispered. His withdrawal from her shocked and frightened her.

'I thought I heard Emma cry out. We'd better go and check up on her. We oughtn't to be doing this, anyway. I promised you I wouldn't, didn't I?'

Susannah bit her lip and admitted huskily, 'I wanted you as well.'

She saw him swallow as though he was in pain.

'Yes. Yes, I know.' His voice was raw and slightly hoarse. 'We're behaving more like a couple of teen-agers than two supposedly mature adults. You seem to have that effect on me.'

'And you on me,' Susannah admitted.

She ached to be back in his arms, but he was right, this was neither the time nor the place. They were here primarily to look after Emma, not to make love. And, besides, when Hazard realised the truth about her... Well, he was right, this was not the place.

'I'll get dressed and go and check on Emma.'

'Come here,' he demanded softly.

She went willingly into his arms, quivering as her breasts brushed against the hardness of his chest. His skin was merely warm now, lacking its earlier heat, their mutual passion subdued as they kissed lingeringly.

'You'd better get dressed.' He released her reluctantly.

Emma wasn't awake, but she was very restless. Restless enough, in fact, for Susannah to call for Hazard to come and look at her as well.

'I think she's running a slight fever. Dr Barnes said that she might, as a result of the exposure.'

'What can we do?'

'Nothing for the moment. Dr Barnes promised to call in the morning to check on her. The best thing we can do now is to let her sleep and keep an eye on her.'

It took a great deal of persuasion before Hazard agreed that he would sleep while Susannah sat up in the chair in Emma's room, keeping an eye on the older woman, and it was only after Susannah promised faithfully to wake him if she was at all worried that he finally agreed.

At four o'clock in the morning, he got up and told Susannah that it was her turn to rest. Emma had woken once, and very groggily asked what was going on. At first, Susannah had been concerned that her fever might have robbed her of all memory of what had happened, but then Emma had quickly put her fears at rest by saying huskily, 'Of course, I remember now. I fell, and you and Hazard are being my Good Samaritans. What time is it? It feels like the middle of the night.' She glanced at her alarm clock. 'It *is* the middle of the night! My dear, you should be in bed...'

'You were a little feverish, and we thought one of us should sit with you. I've made some chicken soup. Would you like some?' Susannah asked, mindful of the fact that Emma had not eaten with them earlier.

'Oh, I couldn't put you to that trouble.'

'It's no trouble at all,' Susannah assured her, and before Emma could demur any further she went downstairs to heat up the soup and make a hot drink.

Emma had just fallen asleep again when Hazard came in and announced that it was Susannah's turn to have some rest.

'I promise you, I'll wake you if I need you,' he told her, propelling her firmly towards the door.

She was tired, the day had been so eventful. Most importantly because of the complete turnaround in her relationship with Hazard, but also because of Emma's accident.

Who would have thought that, less than twenty-four hours ago, she had been dreading the thought of spending a full day with Hazard?

She ought to tell him the truth about herself, but she hated raising the subject, knowing how much he disapproved of her affair with David. Every time the subject cropped up, his face darkened and a frown appeared. He seemed to withdraw slightly from her, and the discovery of her love was too new and precious to be exposed to any harsh winds. And yet the knowledge of her deception worried her conscience like a thorn in tender skin. Soon, she would tell him soon, she promised herself as sleep claimed her.

The sound of voices outside her door woke her. Susannah sat up in bed, disorientated and muzzy-headed, and then realised to her horror how long she had slept. It was almost ten o'clock!

'She's been awake for some time,' she heard Hazard saying. 'She was a little feverish last night, but she seems fine this morning.'

A woman's voice responded. Dr Barnes, Susannah realised, waiting until they had gone into Emma's room before leaping out of bed and hurrying into the bedroom.

She had washed her underwear through the previous night, and it had dried in the heat of the airing cupboard. Even so, she grimaced a little distastefully at the thought of wearing yesterday's shirt.

Emma had told her where to find a new toothbrush. They would have to share, Hazard had suggested. Hazard... Her insides melted with love, her body wantonly weak with longing. If Emma hadn't cried out last night, by now they would be lovers. She shivered sensually, a ripple of sensation stroking over her skin at the memory of his body against her own.

Only the realisation of how cold the bathroom was brought her out of her dreamy state. The boiler must have gone out.

She paused briefly outside Emma's door, and then decided not to go in.

Downstairs, in the kitchen, she saw that Hazard had cleaned out and attempted to light the boiler, apparently unsuccessfully. She looked for and found the flue adjustment, tutting a little as she carefully reconstructed Hazard's rather haphazard fire. With the flue correctly adjusted and the door closed, the fire began to draw properly. Satisfied that it would stay in, she went outside to get more fuel.

When she came back, Hazard and Dr Barnes were standing in the kitchen.

'How on earth did you manage to do that?' Hazard demanded, mock-aggrieved, relieving her of the bucket of fuel. 'I've been trying to get it lit for the past hour.'

'Technique,' she told him with a grin. The look they exchanged was long and explicit. Her face flushed as she knew that, like her, he was remembering last night and how his expertise had set them both on fire.

'Filthy things,' Dr Barnes condemned. 'Give me clean electricity any day.' Ignoring Susannah, she turned to Hazard, placing immaculate pearl-polished fingertips on his arm in a gesture that immediately aroused all Susannah's feminine instincts.

'You really have been marvellous to Emma. Lucy, her niece, is due back later this afternoon. I'll give her a ring and let her know the situation. Look... I'm having a few friends for lunch today, why don't you join us?'

She didn't look at Susannah or include her in the invitation, and Susannah held her breath, wondering what Hazard's response would be.

'Thank you, you're very kind,' he replied pleasantly. 'But I can't really leave Susannah to cope on her own.'

A disparaging, dismissing glance from Dr Barnes's ice-cold blue eyes swept Susannah from head to toe and then dismissed her.

'Why not? She seems extremely capable...'

'Oh, she is,' Hazard agreed smoothly, his voice cooling slightly. 'Very capable.' As he spoke, he reached out and gently tugged Susannah close to his side, holding her there with his arm. The smile he gave her made her insides clench, Dr Barnes forgotten as she turned her face up to his, her eyes radiant with her love.

'Well, if you'll excuse me...' Dr Barnes's voice was touched with frost, her smile taut and not at all pleased. Susannah could even feel it in her heart to feel sorry for her; after all, she was not to blame for being attracted to Hazard. What woman in her right mind would not be?

'That wasn't very kind of you,' Susannah chided him when she had gone.

'What did you want me to do? Accept her invitation?' His eyes teased, knowing her response. 'Mmm...you smell nice.'

'Only of soap.'

'That as well,' he agreed obliquely, bending to murmur in her ear as she frowned her lack of understanding. 'You have a scent that is uniquely your own, a special fragrance that I personally find extremely erotic. *Extremely* erotic,' he repeated huskily, his voice dropping, his hands sliding up over her body to pull her into the strength of his own. 'I hope you dreamed about me last night.'

She had done, shockingly erotic dreams in which she had done and said things she had never imagined herself saying or doing before, and she flushed wildly, instinctively dropping her lashes to cover her eyes, in case he read her thoughts. There were times when she still felt awkward and unsure with him; times when her lack of experience made her feel shy and uncertain.

'I dreamed about you.' Hazard's body moved, hardening into arousal, making her quiver and ache. His hand slid inside her blouse, releasing her breast from the confinement of her bra. She shuddered tensely as his thumb rubbed across her taut nipple. 'Susannah.'

Her name was torn from his lips, the sound smothered against her creamy flesh as he bent his head to savour the tantalising arousal of her body.

A shudder of pleasure shook her. Instinctively, she pressed closer to the hardness of his thighs, her own moving in imploring, seductive enticement against him.

'Hazard!' His name whispered past her lips in a husky plea. His hands moved down over her and she shivered in agonised arousal.

'We can't—not now. Emma's awake and...' Gently, he pushed her away from him, and she fought to mask her disappointment. 'You intoxicate me, do you know that? You're more lethal than a bottle of spirits. When I see you like this...' His eyes darkened as his gaze moved slowly over her trembling mouth and then down to the exposed fullness of her breast.

Susannah held her breath, willing him to take her back in his arms. For a moment, it seemed he would, and then, with a tremendous effort, he gently restored her clothing to its original state.

Susannah wasn't sure which of them shook the most as he fastened her shirt buttons. She rather suspected it was herself.

'When I touch you, I could almost think that I'm the first man to teach you the meaning of physical pleasure.' He grimaced wryly. 'Odd how man's innate chauvinism can catch him out at times.'

'Would you want that ... knowing that you're my first lover?'

The fierce blaze that illuminated his eyes half frightened her. She shook beneath the raw passion of it, and then it died, his eyes going flat and hard as he said tonelessly, 'You're talking myths and fairy stories; the days when a man valued a woman for her virginity are long gone, and so they should be.'

'So you don't mind that...that there have been other men in my life?' she asked uncertainly. She wanted to tell him the truth, but she was frightened of his reaction. Emotionally, he might want to be her first lover, but practically speaking...

'What the hell do you think I am? Of course I mind,' he told her fiercely. 'I'm as jealous as hell at the thought of any other man touching you, but these are the nineteen-eighties, Susannah, and I wouldn't think much of myself as a man if I couldn't accept that there have been other relationships in your life, just as there have in mine.'

'No. It's the fact that one of those relationships was with a married man that you really resent, isn't it?' she asked, groping for the truth, trying to understand what motivated him. 'Hazard, is that because your parents were divorced? Is...'

'Stop it! I don't want to talk about it. For God's sake, Susannah, can't you see that I want to forget that there was ever anyone else in your life? I...I'd prefer not to talk about it.' He turned away from her. 'I'll go and make some coffee.'

Susannah let him go, not daring to even try to reach out and touch him, either physically or emotionally. They had been on the very brink of having their first real quarrel, and she had bungled everything dreadfully. All she had wanted to do was to tell him the truth. But what was the truth? That she had been emotionally but not physically involved with a married man? She was just as culpable as if she *had* had an affair with David, and that was something she never allowed herself to forget. She only had to remember the pitiable state to which his wife had reduced herself, begging her to give him back to her, to be filled with nausea and distaste. She had hated herself then, and she still carried some of that hatred deep inside her like a poison. What she wanted was absolution, but that did not come from man, it came from God. It came from within oneself, she admitted tiredly.

Never, as long as she lived, would she forget David's wife's face. Perhaps *that* was to be her punishment. She had ended the affair just as soon as she had known the truth, but maybe she should have guessed earlier that David was married. She should have known that he was deceiving her.

Her thoughts went round and round in tormented circles, engrossing her to the extent that she physically jumped when Hazard spoke to her. 'Coffee's ready.'

They drank it in silence. Emma, it seemed, had had breakfast earlier. The electricity was back on and Hazard had been able to make her a light meal.

'The flood water has gone down, Joanna Barnes told me, and the forecast for today is very windy but dry, so we shouldn't have any trouble leaving once Emma's niece can confirm that she's able to come and take over.'

Susannah couldn't look at him. Stupidly, tears blurred her eyes. Her hand shook so much, she had to hold on to her mug with both hands.

'I'm sorry.' His gentle words made her throat ache. 'It's just...I suppose I'm not used to opening up about myself with people, and I'm so damned jealous whenever I think of you with someone else. The more I get to know you, the less I'm able to understand how you could get yourself involved in that sort of relationship. You're so uncompromisingly honest, Susannah.'

His voice was rough with suppressed emotion.

'I think we both got a little carried away. Too much emotion too early in the morning,' she said shakily.

'Not to mention the fact that I, for one, am as frustrated as hell,' Hazard agreed bluntly. 'I'd like to take you away somewhere, where I can have you completely to myself. Next weekend, perhaps?'

The rest of the day passed very quickly. Emma insisted on giving them an interview, despite their protests that it could wait until she was feeling better.

A telephone call from her niece confirmed that she would be there later in the afternoon. Hazard and Susannah waited until she arrived.

She was a pleasant, capable-looking woman in her thirties, who quickly took charge and thanked them for coming to her aunt's assistance. 'We keep warning her that it's too remote for her up here, especially in winter, but this was the home she shared with Uncle Harold when he was alive, and she doesn't want to leave it. I can understand why, but Ralph and I worry about her. She was cut off by heavy snowfalls three times last winter, and now this . . .' She shrugged her shoulders. 'But what can you do? I value my own independence, so I sympathise with her.'

As they drove home, Hazard told Susannah that he had a prior commitment for most of Sunday that he couldn't get out of.

'Lunch with our chairman, as a matter of fact,' he added by way of explanation.

'Oh yes, of course. You've known him a long time, haven't you?' She fell silent as he turned to study her, his face cold and shuttered.

'How do you know that?'

Not wanting to admit that he had been the subject of office gossip, she shrugged and fibbed unconvincingly, 'Oh, I can't remember. I must have heard it somewhere . . .'

His eyes were bleak, and Susannah had the feeling that he was furiously angry with her. But why? Because she had mentioned his relationship with Mac? What was there in that to warrant his sudden coldness?

She felt drained and exhausted, too exhausted to have another quarrel with him. They would have to talk about it later, when she felt better able to come to grips with the situation.

They parted outside the door of her flat. Susannah didn't invite him in, and her goodbye was stilted. She turned to push the door open and stiffened as Hazard caught hold of her, spinning her round and plundering her mouth with his with almost frenzied passion.

All her doubts and resentment vanished. She clung eagerly to him. 'Don't invite me to come in,' he groaned against her mouth. 'If I do, I'll probably never leave. You and I need time, Susannah. Time to be alone with one another, with no ghosts intruding between us. Meet me tomorrow night. We'll have dinner together. I should be free by then.'

'I can't,' she told him regretfully. 'I've promised to baby-sit for a friend. It's her wedding anniversary and I can't let her down.'

'No... I understand.' He kissed her again, lingeringly and thoroughly, so that she felt her bones were melting. 'How on earth I'm going to get any work done with you about to distract me, I have no idea!'

From her flat window, Susannah watched him drive away, and she felt as though he had taken a part of her with him.

CHAPTER EIGHT

ON MONDAY morning, Susannah dressed for the office in a very nervous state of mind. She both longed to see Hazard and yet dreaded seeing him, and the fact that they would be meeting as colleagues rather than lovers made it all the more difficult. She felt incredibly nervous about continuing to work closely with him. She frowned, remembering the circumstances surrounding her new position within the magazine. Hazard had *demoted* her! Oh, perhaps not obviously, but she knew that he had. He didn't trust her judgement, and she knew enough about him to know that their new relationship would not change that.

But why had he taken such a harsh attitude towards her? Richard had always been full of praise for her work, so encouraging.

She arrived at work to discover that Hazard would not be coming in. 'He must have rung very early,' Lizzie told her. 'I came in and found a message on the answering machine. Apparently, he's had to fly to New York.'

A tiny, cold finger of doubt reached out and pressed maliciously against Susannah's spine. *Why* had he said nothing to her? *Why* had he not rung her?

She spent the morning typing up the notes from the interview with Emma. It had been fun conducting the interview in a way that would not reveal her real sex. Hazard had allowed her to conduct the interview alone, and she had seen this as a slight softening of his working attitude towards her. However, today, for some reason, the printed words looked flat and lifeless.

She decided to take an early lunch, hoping that the break would send her back to work with renewed zeal.

The rain had stopped over the weekend, but the weather was still far from fine, with a cool, mean little east wind and a depressing layer of monotonous cloud.

Head down against the wind, deep in thought, she apologised automatically as she cannoned into someone.

'Susannah!'

'Richard.' She smiled her pleasure and surprise at seeing him.

'I was just on my way over to the magazine. How are you? Is all going well?'

The temptation to confide in him almost overwhelmed her, and as though he sensed her mood of depression he glanced at his watch and said quickly, 'Look, I'm due at a meeting in fifteen minutes, but I'm staying over in town tonight. Caroline has taken the kids to see her father for a week, and so I decided I might as well get as much work crammed in as I could in her absence. How about having dinner with me tonight?'

Dinner with Richard... Richard, who was Mac's son-in-law, and who might be able to give her more background information about Hazard. Information she was suddenly greedy for, she recognised, subduing the small Aunt-Emily-created voice that warned her she was playing in dangerous waters, and which added sternly that if Hazard wanted her to have such information he would give it to her himself.

She didn't want to listen to such sensible statements, and so, recklessly ignoring them, she nodded. 'I'll pick you up about eight, if that's OK.'

Seeing Richard had done the trick. By the time she got back to work, Susannah felt a resurgence of her normal energy. She rang Emma's niece and asked after the patient, relieved to hear that the older woman was well on the road to recovery. She then got down to working on her article, but every time the phone rang her whole body tensed.

She desperately wanted to hear Hazard's voice. New York—what could have taken him there? She didn't even know when he was due back.

'You're very on edge,' Lizzie commented as five o'clock drew near. 'Something wrong?'

'No... nothing. Did... did Hazard say if he would ring again?' She couldn't look at Lizzie as she asked the question, in case she gave herself away.

The other girl seemed totally unaware of her tension. 'No, he didn't, but I expect he'll get in touch if he thinks there's anything we need to know,' she said comfortably, covering her typewriter and standing up. 'I'm off. How about you?'

'I think I'll hang on for a while. I'm still not entirely happy with this article.'

It wasn't true, but it gave her an excuse to remain in the office, just in case Hazard should ring.

'My, my! Still hard at it,' Claire commented mockingly when she poked her head round the door half an hour later. 'Lucky you, by the way,' she added sarcastically, 'working so close to our very eligible boss. Has he chased you round the desk yet?'

'Don't be ridiculous!' Susannah snapped before she could stop herself.

'It wouldn't exactly be his style, would it? Besides, I hear that these days the boot is very much on the other foot. Or, should I say, the high heel is very much on the other foot? It seems our modern, successful, executive sisters aren't always above demanding, from lesser male colleagues, those favours that used to be a totally male preserve.'

Susannah couldn't see where the conversation was leading, but she knew Claire too well to allow her to see that she was irritating her. There was nothing Claire enjoyed more than tormenting some unfortunate victim into retaliation.

'I think I'll be on my way.' She tidied up her desk and stood up.

'Yes, so must I. Pity Hazard isn't here. I've got two tickets for *La Bohème* tonight. I was going to offer him one.'

'He doesn't like opera.'

The words slipped out unguardedly. Claire's eyebrows rose. 'Really? And how would you know that, darling?'

'He must have mentioned it in passing,' Susannah stammered as carelessly as she could. 'Look, I must go, Claire, I'm going out tonight.'

The last thing she wanted was for the fashion columnist to realise she was in love with Hazard.

She had already discovered how very close-mouthed he was about his private life, and if he thought she had been gossiping about their relationship with someone else ... Wearily, she left the office. She had been apprehensive about seeing him again this morning, but that apprehension had been washed away by the flood of disappointment that had swept over her when she'd realised he wouldn't be there.

New York ... What was he doing there? Who was he with? Jealousy and doubt, two very dangerous and damaging emotions, she recognised, fighting to subdue them. No relationship could thrive healthily when they were present. They were like choking ivy, strangling the life out of love.

It was still cold, the east wind more suited to winter than late summer.

Perhaps she needed a holiday, and that was why she was feeling so down, she reflected, and then fell to daydreaming about some isolated, pale, sandy beach on a tropical island, where she and Hazard were alone.

It was disheartening to come back to life and recognise that she was in London and Hazard in New York.

Richard picked her up at eight as he had promised. He drove her to a small, quiet restaurant that specialised in Italian food.

'I remembered it was your favourite,' he explained as he led her inside.

The restaurant was family-run, small and friendly, the food among the best she had ever tasted, but still the evening felt flat. Richard drew her out skilfully and she found herself confiding in him, telling him of her concern about her demotion.

'I don't think for one moment that Hazard can doubt your ability,' he comforted her kindly. 'He's probably anxious to make sure you don't overstretch yourself too quickly. I saw him at the weekend, as it happens, and he certainly didn't give me the impression that he was concerned about you. How are you getting on with him, apart from that? On a more personal level, for instance?'

'On a personal level?' Susannah shot him a doubtful look, and then, when she saw his face, decided against prevarication. 'I think I'm in love with him. Really in love—nothing like what I felt for David,' she admitted shakily. 'Ridiculous, isn't it? I hardly know him, and yet...'

'I know just what you mean. It was like that with Caro and me. She was everything I didn't want for myself: the boss's daughter, self-willed, intelligent—everything I disliked. I'd come up the hard way and, if I'm honest, I had a bit of a chip on my shoulder. The first time I met her I thought she was the snootiest bitch I'd ever set eyes on, and she went out of her way to go on making sure I felt like that.'

'So what happened?' Susannah pressed him, curious, in spite of Aunt Emily's upbringing that stipulated that one must never ask others personal questions.

'Mac happened,' Richard told her wryly. 'He kept on throwing us together until one day the light dawned.'

'You love her very much, don't you?' Susannah asked softly.

'More than I thought it possible for me to love any woman,' he agreed. 'The way I feel about Caroline changed me a great deal. Until then, I'd been very scornful about emotion. My own parents separated when I was quite young...but enough about me. You're in love with Hazard, you say.'

'And he says he feels the same way about me.'

'So what's bothering you?'

'I know so little about him,' she told him expressively. 'He's so...so guarded whenever I mention his past. It's as though he wants to draw a veil over it.'

'And you think I might be able to lift that veil? I'm sorry, Susannah,' Richard replied, shaking his head. 'I can't. You must see that,' he told her gently.

'I...I...know, or at least I've heard that he was practically brought up by Mac,' she faltered slightly as Richard's expression grew stern.

'Susannah, Hazard himself is really the person you should ask about this.'

'I've tried to but, every time the subject crops up, it's as though he's deliberately shutting me out.'

Richard looked at her thoughtfully. 'You're a sensitive person, too sensitive, perhaps, to make a truly successful reporter—for that you need an ability to close yourself off from other people's feelings, and you can't do that. Hazard, on the other hand...' He paused, as though seeking the right words. 'Hazard has taught himself not just to block himself off from the feelings of others, but to block himself off from his own as well.'

He caught her shocked exclamation of distress and shook his head. 'I'm afraid it's true, Susannah, and if your relationship with him is to have any real basis you must accept that. I can't tell you any more without betraying confidences that aren't mine to give. You say you're *in love* with Hazard. I don't doubt it. He's a very charismatic man, but do you *love* him? I hope so, my dear, because he's a man who needs the kind of love you have to give very badly. It's up to you, Susannah. *You* must find a way through the barriers, because I doubt that he'll ever let them down voluntarily. Sometimes, things happen to us that have such a traumatic effect on our lives that we can't set them aside...'

'Are you saying that's what happened to Hazard? Something so traumatic...'

'I've already said more than enough,' Richard told her. 'Think very hard before you commit yourself to him, Susannah, because breaking down those barriers won't be easy.'

'I'll find a way,' she told him, and in her naïveté she foolishly believed it would be that simple; that she only had to be determined and strong enough, and Hazard would voluntarily put aside his defences.

They had been talking for so long that the restaurant was virtually empty. It was cold outside, and Susannah was glad to get into the warmth of Richard's car.

'Very county,' she teased him, noting that he had changed his saloon for a larger estate model, complete with dog-grille in the back.

Richard grinned at her a little shamefacedly, 'You know, for years I've fought to stay what I was essentially before I married Caroline—a working newspaper man—but now...' He shook his head self-mockingly. 'It's been less than a month, and already I feel like a country hick in London, and what's more, I hate this city. I've seen more of the kids in recent weeks than I've seen of them in as many years. If someone had told me how content I'd be with my life now, I'd have denied it. What I'm trying to tell you, Susannah, is that all of us have within us the capacity for change; none of us knows ourself quite as well as we think.'

'You mean, the leopard can change its spots?' Susannah asked drily.

'Perhaps, given the right incentive.'

They were outside her flat now and, as he stopped the car, he leaned across her and planted an elder-brotherly kiss on her cheek.

'I'll give you one piece of encouragement. Mac prefers his executives to be married. He says it's because it steadies them down. *Ties* them down is probably closer to the truth! A man with a mortgage and a family isn't as likely to give up his job as one who's completely free.'

'Thanks,' Susannah responded waspishly. 'If my relationship with Hazard ever gets that far, the last thing I want is to be married because Mac approves.'

Richard laughed at her. 'And Hazard is the last man to allow himself to be manoeuvred in such a way. I'd better go. I promised I'd give Caro a ring when I got in.'

Impulsively, Susannah reached out and hugged him. 'Thanks!'

He wasn't old enough to be a substitute father, but she felt a welling of warm affection towards him that had something of the emotion she suspected she might have felt for her long dead male parent.

'It won't be easy,' he warned her. 'Sometimes you're going to think that you're the one doing all the giving, and you will be; people are like that when their feelings have been brutalised the way Hazard's have. Be patient, Susannah!'

It was frustrating to have so much hinted at and yet have it remain a mystery. What was it that lay in Hazard's past that he refused to talk about?

There was only one way she was going to find out, she recognised. As she unlocked the door to her flat, she wished that he was with her. She badly needed the reassurance of his physical presence. If only he was here to take her in his arms and sweep away all her doubts!

It was gone twelve; she might as well go to bed. Where was Hazard now? What was he doing?

Someone knocked at her door and her heart leapt. The joy that stormed through her as she opened it and saw Hazard standing there just couldn't be expressed. She wanted to run to him and fling her arms round him, but the shock of seeing him there, when she had believed he was still in New York, held her tongue-tied and motionless.

'So it's all over between you and your married lover, is it?' he said harshly, through gritted teeth, striding into the flat and slamming the door behind him.

His face was contorted and dark with rage, and now that the spell of his unexpected appearance had been broken by the fury in his voice, Susannah could see that he looked tired and drawn.

'You couldn't wait to run to him could you? You couldn't wait to be back in his arms! Have you no conscience? No thought for the destructive misery you're causing? Do his wife and family really count for so little?'

'Hazard . . .' she broke in, shocked.

'Cut out the acting,' he demanded bitterly. 'It won't do any good. I saw you with my own eyes in his car. You two-timing little bitch . . . You really tried to play me for a fool, didn't you?'

'Hazard, what are you talking about?' Her head was spinning, her body weak with shock and dismay.

'You know damn well what I'm talking about. Your affair with Richard! The moment Caroline told me that she was concerned for her marriage, I guessed what was happening. After all, it isn't anything out of the ordinary, is it? The keen young assistant, the experienced older man. I don't suppose you ever gave a single thought for his wife and family. They just didn't matter, did they?'

'You . . . you think I'm having an affair with *Richard*?'

Susannah was standing up, and she had to grab hold of the back of the chair to prevent herself from collapsing with shock.

'No, I don't *think* it, I *know* it!' Hazard shot back at her. 'I've just seen the two of you outside in his car. God, you couldn't wait, could you? The moment my back was turned. A pretty fool you must think me! All those soft protestations, all that remorse, and all the time——' He looked at her with hard eyes. 'I suppose you even guessed what I was trying to do?'

'Trying to do?' Susannah felt as though she had walked into a nightmare. She had no idea why on earth Hazard should think she was having an affair with Richard. She was trying to tell him as much, but, every time she tried, he shouted her down with some fresh piece of invective.

'Oh, come on, don't play the innocent! You obviously guessed I was trying to break the two of you up by pretending I wanted you myself.'

An awful coldness seized her, chilling her to the bone. She stood like a statue, barely able to even breathe. Her lungs felt congested, her heart an icy lump of pain lodged somewhere deep inside her.

She saw Hazard frown, observing it as though it was something remote and unconnected with her own pain.

'You can cut out the injured innocent act. We both know it means nothing.'

She didn't hear him. Her thought processes, frozen along with the rest of her senses, came slowly to life. 'What do you mean, pretending you want me?'

Her voice seemed to come from a distance, as though someone else had spoken. She looked at him with pain-shadowed eyes, her mouth stiff with the agony she was trying to control.

'Oh, come on! The farce is over, Susannah. You know quite well what I mean.'

'No... No, I'm afraid I don't.'

An odd expression rippled across his hard face, doubt flickering momentarily in his eyes, and then they too hardened, cold and hostile as they surveyed her agonised pallor.

'You're having an affair with Richard,' he told her contemptuously. 'When Caroline pleaded with me to take the job Mac was offering me, she told me that her marriage depended on it. Caroline is the closest thing I have to a sister. She's never asked me for anything before—not *anything*!'

Susannah closed her eyes and tried to think rationally, while her emotions cried out to her for something to take away the pain. How could she think while she felt like this? How could she do anything other than submit to the agony his words were inflicting?

'Caroline told you that Richard and I were having an affair?' She couldn't believe it.

'Not in so many words. She didn't need to. When she told me that she was having marital problems, I knew immediately there must be another woman involved. It didn't take much intelligence to work out that *you* must be the woman. When I saw them before I took over from him, Richard couldn't stop himself from singing your praises.'

'And...when you saw me...at the party, you knew who I was?'

'Not immediately, but when you started talking about your married lover, I started to suspect.'

It was all a nightmare. It had to be! She wanted to tell him that he was wrong, but pain burned in her chest, making it almost impossible for her to speak.

'And you were determined to come between me and Richard right from the start?'

'I was determined to break you up, whatever it took, yes,' he told her uncompromisingly.

'And...and last weekend...everything you said to me then...that was all a...a pretence?'

His lashes dropped, shadows slanting over harsh cheekbones as he turned slightly away from her. 'You seemed to be attracted to me.' He shrugged, and the smile he gave her wasn't a pleasant one. 'I thought it was a good opportunity to pretend that I was equally attracted to you and detach you from Richard, but it seems you were even more devious than I thought. Tell me something,' he demanded, taking hold of her and shaking her savagely, 'did you tell him how close we came to making love?'

This *couldn't* be happening, but it was, and Susannah was too overwhelmed by the shock of it to defend herself. Besides, what did it matter? Hazard cared nothing for her; he had just told her so.

'Well, did you...?'

Did she what? She stared up at him with bruised, shocked eyes.

'God! Even now you can't stop putting on the injured innocent air, can you?' he breathed bitterly. 'Do you know, there were moments last weekend when you almost had me convinced that I was practically the first man ever to have touched you... What will it take to make you give him up?' he demanded abruptly. 'How much?'

The pain inside her body couldn't be contained. Her throat was too taut to give voice to anything more than a small, searing moan.

'Perhaps I'm going about this the wrong way. Perhaps it would be easier to make *him* give *you* up. What would it take, I wonder?' His eyes darkened mercilessly. 'I wonder how he'd feel about the thought of you making love with another man. With me, for instance?'

Somewhere deep inside Susannah a scream of denial built up, but it couldn't be voiced. She had gone beyond that, retreated somewhere where no more pain could touch her. She felt Hazard pick her up, and knew he intended to make good his threat. Her body was limp and unmoving in his arms, her eyes dark, empty pools of nothing as he laid her on the small single bed.

'How will he like the sight of your body bearing the signs of another man's caresses?' Hazard muttered furiously, looming over her.

His hands were on the zip of her dress, tugging it downwards. Susannah shivered as she felt the cold air brush her skin.

'Tell me you'll give him up.'

She closed her eyes and turned her head, knowing there was nothing she could say. It would be the final terrible destruction of what she had believed there was between them; the ultimate blasphemy, a parody of what their lovemaking should have been. Deep down inside her soul, a tiny part of her wanted him to make her hate him, and so she didn't resist as his hands found her skin and slid away the protection of her clothes.

'Give me your word that you'll give him up, and I'll stop this right now.'

Her word. He demanded her *word*, when she had been prepared to give him so much more?

Let him do what he liked, she no longer cared.

She kept her head averted and heard him mutter savagely, 'So cold and remote, but you weren't like this the other night, were you? Shall I make you burn for me like that again, Susannah? Shall I make you cry out for my hands, my body?'

She felt his breath against her skin and tensed, but he didn't touch her mouth. Instead, his lips feathered across the satin smoothness of her shoulder, his fingers stroking softly against her skin.

'One way or another, I'll make you give him up, you know that, don't you?' he threatened softly.

She heard the words, and yet they meant nothing. Her frozen flesh lay dormant beneath his touch. She felt the stillness invade his body, and didn't resist the hand that turned her face towards his own so that he could look into her eyes.

His glittered beneath the thick darkness of his lashes. She could feel the heat of his rage, but it meant nothing to her. Her eyes mirrored the frozen stillness of her body.

'Say something, damn you!'

He seemed to know exactly how to coax her vulnerable flesh into arousal. Her mind writhed back from the humiliation he was enforcing. She closed her eyes against the sight of his dark head against her breasts, of his hands splayed out across the quivering swell of her stomach.

'After tonight, no matter who touches you, you're always going to remember this,' he told her thickly, his eyes glittering up at her as his hands roamed her body with insolent possession.

If she hadn't loved him, it wouldn't be like this; it was her love for him that made her weak, just as it was his hatred of her that made him strong. Hatred must be just as powerful a stimulant as love, Susannah decided brokenly, feeling the hardening of his body against her, shocked by his arousal when she knew how much he despised her. It was so hard to stem the swell of feeling building inside her; so very, very hard to maintain the tense stillness of her body, when every nerve-ending wanted to respond openly to his touch.

'Such self-control!' he marvelled tauntingly. 'I wonder what it will take to break it? And I shall break it, Susannah. I shall break it, and hear you cry out my name. And the next time you go to your lover, it will be me you remember!'

He'd do anything to break up her relationship with Richard, he had said. Her body quivered and Susannah saw him smile.

'See, you can't fight me for ever. You're too sensual . . . too aware.'

Her frail control broke under the invasive stroke of his tongue. She heard herself cry out and reach for him, wanting him deep within her, but already he was moving away. Abruptly he stood up, looking down into her vulnerable face, and then very slowly he bent and picked up her dress and threw it to her.

'Break off your relationship with Richard, otherwise I'll make sure he knows not just about last weekend, but about this as well. And, believe me, I shan't miss out on a single detail!'

He hated her so much?

'Nothing to say?'

She couldn't speak at all. Some sort of temporary paralysis seemed to have attacked her vocal cords.

'You've got until the weekend to break off with him,' he told her curtly. 'I'm going now. Sweet dreams.'

How long she simply sat there, clutching her dress, Susannah never knew. Time seemed to pass, but she wasn't really aware of it. She heard clocks chime, but the sound only impinged faintly on her bruised mind. She knew she was cold, but she made no attempt to cover herself. She knew she was hurt, but she made no attempt to stifle the pain. Some sort of blankness seemed to have come over her; some sort of semi-comatose state that mercifully distanced her from anything approaching reality.

Outside the windows of her flat, the city started to come to life. Her alarm went off, and she stared at it as though she had never seen it before. No sense of urgency to get dressed and go to work possessed her; no sense of anything other than the containment of the dreadful pain she knew lay somewhere, waiting for her.

Time passed. Her phone rang. She heard it, but didn't move. An awareness that there were things she ought to do touched her vaguely and then disappeared, but she was so cold that she pulled on her dressing-gown, almost absent-mindedly.

Towards lunch time, she heard the doorbell's peal. She looked numbly in the direction of the sound, but didn't move.

Some time later, she heard the outer door open. High-heeled feet tapped their way impatiently to her room. The door was pushed open, and Mamie stood on the threshold, irritation giving way to shocked concern as she looked at the girl on the bed.

'Susannah...'

Unfocusing, pained eyes turned towards her.

'Oh, my God, what's happened?'

Suddenly Susannah's mind snapped back to reality. There was no way she could tell Mamie the truth. A need to protect herself overcame her mental agony, a fierce, driving need to conceal from curious eyes all that had happened. This was a pain that couldn't be shared, not with anyone.

'Susannah, what's going on? I went to collect you for lunch, and they told me at the magazine that you hadn't been in. Are you ill?'

Her gaze took in the rumpled bed, and Susannah's frozen pose.

'Why didn't you answer the door? I had to go down and get a pass key. Susannah, what's going on?'

'Nothing.' Somehow, she summoned a stiff smile. 'Nothing...'

'Don't give me that! Some man's done this to you... What happened, honey? Come on, you can tell me...'

She had to speak, otherwise Mamie would be leaping to all sorts of wrong conclusions.

'No... nothing like that.'

'Then...'

'Please, Mamie, I don't want to talk about it... Is it too late to have lunch? I can get ready quite quickly.'

The last thing she wanted was food, but instinct told her that she had to deflect Mamie's questions. If she didn't, Mamie would probe and pry until she had dragged every last humiliating scrap of information out of her.

'Well...' For once, the American looked nonplussed.

'Where shall we eat?' Susannah pressed.

'Well, if you're sure you feel well enough...'

'I'm fine. Why don't you wait for me in the sitting-room?'

A little to her surprise, Mamie agreed and, although she did try to bring up the subject again over lunch, Susannah forestalled her, talking determinedly instead about other matters. By the time she finally parted from the older woman, Susannah was exhausted. She couldn't stay in London, she decided as she went home. She needed somewhere quiet and tranquil, where she could come to terms with the agony burning inside her. She needed a bolt-hole. She needed sanctuary—somewhere to hide and heal.

She thought of Aunt Emily and dismissed the idea. No, she couldn't go home. So where, then? Where?

Almost without thinking, she found she was gathering clothes together, folding them, putting them into cases. She put the cases in her car, locked the flat behind her, and she had taken the road that led northwards before she recognised exactly where she was heading. Susannah reached the farmhouse late at night, reality breaking through the icy darkness of her despair when she realised what she had done. The kitchen door opened and Emma's niece, Lucy, came out.

Susannah climbed wearily out of her car.

'My goodness, what on earth are you doing up here?'

Susannah started to walk towards her, and then, disconcertingly, she felt the ground tilt. From somewhere, she heard a familiar, concerned voice, and then nothing.

When she came round, she was already inside the farmhouse, two concerned faces peering down at her.

Reality hit her then, breaking through the control she had used to force it aside. She started to shake, a pain too intense for tears tearing at her. 'I . . .'

'Lucy is just going to make us all a cup of tea,' Emma said calmly. As though she had received some signal, her niece got up and left them.

'Don't try and talk now,' Emma suggested quietly. 'I've experienced enough pain of my own in my life to know something of what you're suffering. We'll talk later, when you're ready.'

'I...I shouldn't have come here, imposing myself on you like this. I don't know really why I did.' Susannah's bewilderment showed in her voice.

'My dear, I assure you it's no imposition. You're more than welcome. Now, come closer to the fire. It's a chilly night.'

Gradually, over the next few days, she managed to tell Emma something, but not all, of what had happened. That last humiliating scene...that was something that could never, ever be told. It was burned deep into her soul and could never be erased. That he should think so badly of her...

A letter had been typed and sent to *Tomorrow*, handing in her notice. She badly needed an assistant, to help her with research and to master her word processor, Emma had told her, and somehow or other Susannah had found herself being persuaded to stay.

Emma's niece smiled thankfully and explained that, if Susannah stayed, she would be able to go back to her family. Before she knew it, Susannah had been at the farmhouse for almost a week.

Shock and pain did strange things to the human mind and body, she was discovering. Time had become a fluid rather than a rigid commodity. Sometimes, seconds stretched into hours when she lay awake at night, remembering and longing for sleep; sometimes, hours could simply disappear, melting into minutes as she stared unseeingly into space.

One day she would forget Hazard, she was determined on it; but first she would have to remember him, and that was what she was afraid of and what her mind shrank from so persistently.

CHAPTER NINE

THE days drifted into weeks, and the weeks into one month, and then almost two, and slowly a new pattern of living emerged. No one from the magazine knew where Susannah was. She had written to her aunt, saying that she had changed her job, and her resignation from the magazine had been posted in London, having first been forwarded to Emma's publishers.

The two of them got on well together. Emma had asked her once what she would do if Hazard should contact her, and Susannah had shaken her head and told her quietly, 'That will never happen.'

'Oh, I think you're wrong,' Emma corrected her. 'Once he learns the truth...'

'He won't learn it.'

'I think he will. Our cruellest wrong judgements of people have an unpleasant way of rebounding on us. Think about it,' she urged when Susannah looked doubtful. 'Have you never made even a mental critical judgement of someone, and then discovered later that you were wrong?'

Forced to concede that she was right, Susannah nevertheless remained obdurate that Hazard would not contact her.

'But if he does?' Emma persisted.

The tormented shudder that went through the too-thin body of the girl seated opposite her told its own story, and Emma did not press her any further.

Emma's latest book was going well. She swore that having Susannah working for her made all the difference. It was set in Yorkshire during the Wars of the Roses, a family saga that needed a good deal of research, and Susannah found herself becoming very much more familiar with the area as she accompanied Emma on her research trips.

York was an undeniably beautiful city but, as with everything these days, she saw it from a distance, as though an impenetrable glass wall stood between her and the rest of the world. She knew she needed that glass wall. It protected her from reality and from pain. She knew also that Emma watched her and worried about her. On the surface she functioned perfectly normally, but beneath it her emotions were in chaos. She dreamed constantly about Hazard, confused, sometimes frightening dreams, when she saw him coming towards her and she flew ecstatically towards him, only to tense and stop as she saw his face and read the hatred in it.

Midway through November, an unfamiliar estate car, bearing new registration plates, pulled up outside the farmhouse. Emma had a large circle of friends, and Susannah, who saw the car arrive, hurried down to intercept the visitor, knowing that Emma was tussling with a particularly recalcitrant chapter of her new book.

She opened the door without waiting for the visitor to knock, and then froze as she saw Richard's familiar figure striding towards her.

He stopped when he saw her, apparently as shocked by the sight of her as she was by the sight of him.

'So you *are* here, after all!'

'You've been looking for me?'

'Everywhere we could think of. This was one of the first places we tried, but we were told you weren't here. I was in York on business, and it was only an impulse that maybe Emma King had heard something from you, after all, that brought me up here. Susannah, you're too thin ... Can we go inside and talk?' he begged when she made no immediate response. He saw the pain and fear darken her eyes and stepped towards her. 'Please, Susannah. It's important.'

She wanted to refuse, but the lassitude that overcame her so easily these days engulfed her, and she could do nothing other than turn listlessly towards the kitchen. Emma was always complaining that she didn't eat enough, perhaps that was why she constantly felt so weak, but food had so little appeal, all she really wanted was escape ... escape and oblivion.

'What was it you wanted to talk to me about, Richard?'

She heard him give a faint sigh.

'Susannah, you must know.' When she continued to remain silent, her gaze shifting from him into space, he said quietly, 'Hazard has told us everything.'

She made no response, but a pulse thudded betrayingly in her throat, her whole body tensing. She started to get up, and immediately Richard crossed over to her, gently pushing her back into her chair.

'No, please, you must listen to me.'

'Has Hazard asked you to speak to me?' Suddenly her voice was fierce, anger darkening her eyes.

'He's in America at the moment, and he doesn't know I'm here. Susannah, you can guess how appalled both Caroline and I were when we discovered that Hazard thought you and I were having an affair. We put him right immediately, of course. He refused to believe it at first.'

'I'm sure he did,' Susannah agreed bitterly.

'Yes, but try to understand... There are extenuating circumstances.'

He broke off as her acid laughter interrupted him.

'You're asking *me* to make allowances?' Her voice cracked slightly, registering her disbelief. Suddenly her protective shield splintered, leaving her open to the pain of what he was saying. Like blood returning to numbed limbs, she felt the agony of her surging emotions. Anger burned through her. How dare Richard come here and ask her to understand?

'Susannah, please hear me out. Not so long ago, you told me you loved Hazard.'

He saw her flinch, but pressed on determinedly. 'I'm asking you in the name of that love to listen to me now. For your own sake, if nothing else... Do you think I can't see what's happened to you? Do you want to live like this for the rest of your life, carrying around a burden of bitterness and pain? Do you want to make the same mistakes as Hazard?'

That caught her attention, and she stared at him, her face set. Taking her silence as her agreement to listening, Richard went on quietly, 'Once, you asked me about Hazard's past, but I didn't tell you. Perhaps I should have done, but at the time...' He shrugged tiredly. 'I'm going to tell you now, though, Susannah. For your sake, not for Hazard's,' he added grimly before she could interrupt. 'Hazard's father was a very successful Australian businessman. He was also a rather vain man, or so Mac has told me. When Hazard was eight years old, his father became involved with a woman who worked for him. He left Hazard's mother for her. It's a common enough story, but Hazard's mother couldn't face what had happened. She tried to commit suicide. Hazard found her when he came home from school. She had tried to slash her wrists.'

Richard smiled grimly as he caught Susannah's small gasp.

'Yes, not a very pleasant scene to greet an impressionable eight-year-old. They left Australia, supposedly for a new start in the States but, to cut a long story short, Hazard's mother's mental condition kept on deteriorating. Oh, there were long periods when she was perfectly normal, and then something would happen—she'd become intensely depressed and there would be another attempted suicide.

'Mac could see what was happening. He begged her to allow Hazard to live with him; he tried to tell her that what she was doing to her son wasn't healthy, but she always refused. His concern over his mother quite naturally isolated Hazard from his own peer group. Mac says that he's always been very proud and independent, wouldn't accept any financial help from him, not even to help him get through college.

'At one time, Mac and Hazard's father had been partners, but after the divorce they split the business and Mac moved to the States. Although Hazard's father did very well for himself financially, he never sent Hazard so much as a birthday or Christmas present, and of course, in her saner periods, Hazard's mother blamed his second wife.

'You can see what I'm trying to tell you, can't you, Susannah? Wrong though he was about the affair he thought you and I were having, Hazard acted only as he's been programmed to act since childhood.'

'Yes, I can see that.' Her voice was completely toneless.

Yes, she *could* see and understand now why Hazard had leapt to the absurd conclusion that she and Richard were having an affair. She had mentioned a married lover, after all, and, knowing what she now did, it was only to be expected that the moment Caroline mentioned marriage problems he should assume there was another woman involved.

She, of course, had never mentioned David by name, wanting only to put the whole sorry business behind her, never dreaming what Hazard thought.

'Caroline is distraught with guilt,' Richard went on. 'She had no idea when she begged Hazard to take the job with *Tomorrow* that he would think our marriage was being sabotaged by another woman. Mac feels very much to blame as well. He wanted Hazard over here because he's grooming him to take over from him eventually—I can tell you that, now that you no longer work for the magazine. Hazard refused—he said he wanted to make his own way to the top. Mac was bitterly disappointed. He considers that Hazard is the best man there is to take over from him, and so do I.'

He saw Susannah's face and smiled. 'Oh, yes, I do... I'm a very able lieutenant, but I don't want to be the captain. Anyway, to return to my story, Caroline used emotional pressure on Hazard to get him to take the job, but the marital problems she mentioned were those caused by the fact that she wanted to live in the country, and my job was keeping me in town. She says it never crossed her mind that Hazard would think I was involved in an affair. With hindsight, of course, she realises that she should.'

'How . . . how did it all come out?' Susannah asked him, curious in spite of herself, and then bitterly regretting the question as she saw the gleam of triumph in his eyes. She shouldn't have asked, she should simply have listened and then sent him away.

'Hazard had been over to New York. The sanatorium, where his mother now lives, had telephoned him. She'd had a heart attack, and they thought he should know. Caroline rang him to find out how she was. Whether it was what he said to her, or the fact that he sounded drunk, I'm not sure, but anyway she was concerned enough about him to insist on going to see him.'

'When was this?' Susannah asked him.

Richard frowned, and then mentioned a date.

The day after Hazard had come to see her. Her heart thumped painfully, so many memories that she didn't want crowding in on her.

'When we got to his apartment, we found him out cold on the sofa, a bottle of whisky on the floor beside him. When he eventually came round, the whole story came out, rather disjointedly at first. I think he was too shocked to see us to hold anything back, although later, whenever Caroline tried to bring it up, he cut her off immediately. He tried to find you, Susannah . . . to apologise for misjudging you.'

'It's over, Richard, and I don't want to talk about it. Nor do I want to see him.' She saw that he was about to speak and checked him, saying evenly, 'Did he tell you that he deliberately allowed me to think he was in love with me, solely in order to break up the relationship he thought I had with you?'

Richard looked away from her. 'Yes. Yes. He did.'

'Then I'm sure you understand why I don't want to see him again.'

There was a long silence, and then Richard said quietly, 'Are you sure you won't change your mind?'

'I don't want to see him, Richard. Not now—not ever. I'm glad you've explained to me why he thought you and I were having an affair. That, I can understand. I can even understand his concern for Caroline...'

'You can understand, but you can't forgive, is that it, Susannah?' Richard asked her.

She got up and walked away from him, staring out of the window. Forgive. Was that what she was supposed to do? Smile and say, yes I forgive him? How could she, when her whole body still ached at the memory of him she had? She loved him, and a love like hers couldn't just be cut off, dammed up without causing pain.

She heard the squeak of Richard's chair as he pushed it back. He came to stand alongside her.

'He's a changed man, Susannah. A broken man, you might say. You've made him re-evaluate all the principles on which he's lived his life. The discovery that you are completely innocent...'

'But I'm not.' She turned and looked at him, tears of anger and pain shimmering in her eyes. 'I'm not innocent, Richard. I was involved with a married man—you know that.' She gave a bitter laugh. 'Why don't you tell him that? I'm sure it will make it much easier for him to cope with his guilt.'

'Susannah . . .'

'No, please go, Richard. I'm . . . I'm tired.'

'Can I tell him where you are?'

She looked at him with hard eyes. 'No! I've already told you, Richard, I don't want to see or hear from him ever again.'

For a moment, Susannah thought he was going to try to persuade her to change her mind. Then, with a tired shrug, he shook his head.

'You know your own feelings I suppose, but remember, Susannah, pride makes a cold bedfellow.'

Maybe it did, but she would prefer it to the acid, burning humiliation that was her constant companion, Susannah thought miserably as she watched Richard drive away. He had been disappointed in her, she knew.

When Emma came into the kitchen half an hour later, she found her guest hunched over in a chair, a silent glissade of tears glittering against her pale skin.

She had been waiting for this moment, praying that it would come, and with it the release of Susannah's pent-up emotion; but, now that it had, she found herself more concerned than she had been before. There was something so despairing and agonised about that silent fall of tears that Emma found herself wishing that the man who was the cause of them was here to witness the destruction he had wrought.

It was evening before Susannah had herself under enough control to tell Emma about Richard's visit.

'What will you do if Hazard comes to see you?' Emma asked quietly.

'Why should he want to? What is there left to say?'

'Oh, he will want to.'

Yes, she was right, Susannah recognised. His pride would demand that of him. She laughed sourly. How relieved he would be to discover that he had been right about her, after all, and that she *had* been involved in an affair with a married man.

She said as much to Emma, and the older woman's eyes darkened in sympathy.

'My dear, you were drawn into that situation with lies and deceit. No one would dream of blaming you. *You* were the victim. I think you should see him,' she went on calmly. 'Until you do, you'll never be free to put the past behind you.'

The problem was, she didn't want to put it behind her, Susannah realised. She wanted to remember for always the pain of Hazard's deception. That way, she would never have to suffer such pain again.

Several days later, the phone rang while they were both working in Emma's study. Emma picked up the receiver, and Susannah saw her glance at her and then heard her say, 'I'm afraid I'll have to ring you back. I'm rather busy right now.'

She wrote down a number.

As she replaced the receiver, she made a wry face.

'A magazine interview. I'll ring them back this afternoon. By the way, did you say you were going into the village this morning?'

'Yes. We need stamps, and the bank will be open.'

'Oh, yes... There are one or two other things we could do with as well.' She gave Susannah a list, and then suggested, 'Why don't you go now? I'm a bit bogged down at the moment.'

The first draft of Emma's novel was finished and with her publishers, and she was now involved in plotting out a sequel to it. Knowing that Emma liked to be alone to tussle out problems with her characters, Susannah got up and picked up the list.

Susannah was in the village for almost an hour. There was a long queue both in the post office and at the bank. When she got back, Emma was in the kitchen. She seemed nervy and on edge.

'I have to go to London tomorrow. My publishers have been on. They want to discuss the draft.'

'I'm sure they must like it,' Susannah comforted her. 'I couldn't put it down.'

'Yes . . . Will you be all right here on your own? I shan't be gone more than a couple of days.'

A couple of days! This would be the first time she had stayed at the farmhouse on her own. What was there to worry about? Susannah chided herself. She was twenty-four, not fourteen.

'I'll be fine. I could drive over to York tomorrow and get down to that research.'

'Oh, no!' Emma looked dismayed. 'I mean, I think I'd prefer you to stay here . . . I don't like the house being left empty for too long. We can go to York together when I get back.'

Feeling a little hurt that Emma perhaps didn't trust her to do the research on her own, Susannah forced herself not to betray her feelings. She was becoming far too sensitive and emotional, she warned herself.

Emma's trip to London necessitated a pre-dawn start. She protested that there was no need for Susannah to get up with her, and Susannah refrained from saying that she was invariably awake at that time anyway. Sleep was something that had become elusive these days, and when she did sleep her dreams were so full of Hazard that she often felt more exhausted when she woke from them than before she went to sleep.

The house felt empty without Emma.

She spent the morning industriously cleaning the kitchen, and then typing up Emma's latest notes. The chores were something they shared between them, and working in the large, comfortable kitchen was something Susannah always enjoyed.

At lunch time, she was surprised to discover that she actually felt hungry. She made herself an omelette and ate it at the kitchen table while reading a magazine. Over a cup of coffee, she tried to finish the article she had been reading, but images of Hazard here in the kitchen with her kept on intruding.

Had she come up here in her desperate flight from London and reality because this was the place where she had been so happy?

Although she hadn't wanted to, she had spent a good deal of time mulling over what Richard had said to her. His revelations about Hazard's childhood had shocked her, but she had tried to banish the compassion she had felt. Hazard's determination to protect Caroline's marriage she could understand, but his means of achieving it she could not.

She got up, moving tensely, hugging her arms round her too-slender body. It was so much colder up here, and she felt it. Outside, grey clouds gathered on the horizon. Only last week Emma had mentioned

Christmas. It seemed she normally spent the holiday with her niece.

Susannah had not made any plans, although normally she went home to her aunt. Both she and Hazard were, in their separate ways, victims of an upbringing that was out of step with modern life but, while her aunt's sternness had been motivated only by the highest intentions and her belief that she was doing the right thing, Hazard's mother was obviously a very sick woman mentally. Susannah bit her lip, not wanting to dwell on what Hazard himself must have suffered. She didn't *want* to sympathise with him. She wanted to block herself off from all knowledge of his pain; she wanted to forget him.

But that was impossible!

She was in the study when she heard the car. She went to the front door, only to realise that whoever it was must have driven round the back, and by the time she had reached the back door the driver was walking into the kitchen.

She was totally unprepared for meeting him, the sudden cessation of all movement within her body freezing her to a statue as Hazard walked towards her.

'Susannah.'

The harshly familiar sound of her name on his lips, as though he found the very saying of her name acutely painful, woke from her tormented trance. She stepped back as he came towards her, putting the length of the table between them, and then hanging on to the solid edge of it as she felt the weakness invade her body.

'Susannah, please, I have to speak to you.'

'Richard's already said it all, Hazard,' she told him quietly. 'There's nothing more for you to say.'

He shuddered, and her eyes widened as they registered his pain; he looked pale, and thinner, too. He put his hand out, as though he was going to implore her to change her mind.

'Darling, please, please let me talk to you.'

His voice, raw with longing, penetrated her defences. Unwillingly, she found that she was looking at him, her eyes meeting the grim despair in his. She hadn't wanted to look at him, knowing it would weaken her.

She started to shake, and then she registered that hoarse 'darling', and her skin changed colour, her eyes darkening with pain and rage.

'Please, Susannah, tell me you forgive me for misjudging you. I've been driven nearly out of my mind. I . . .'

She couldn't bear to see him like this, humbling himself, his face white with agony. She didn't want to listen to any more. It hurt her too much. Turning her back on him, she said huskily, 'I forgive you. Now, will you please go?'

She could hardly breathe. With every pulse beat, she half expected to feel him touching her, but he didn't and the silence lengthened, pulsating heavily between them.

At last he spoke, his voice devoid of all emotion. 'Do you really want me to go?'

It caught her raw nerves at their most vulnerable. She spun round, her eyes glittering with resentment and pain.

'No! No, I want you to stay and humiliate me all over again! Of course I want you to go, and I wish you hadn't come here in the first place. And, anyway, you weren't so far wrong about me, you know. There *was* a married man...'

'Yes... Yes, I know.'

He *knew*? Richard, of course.

She heard his footsteps on the tiled floor, not coming towards her but retreating. He was doing what she had asked. He was leaving.

She felt the gust of cold air as the back door opened, and her whole body tensed in anguish as she fought to suppress the plea rising inside her.

The door closed. The car engine fired.

She couldn't bear to see him drive away, and so she fled instead to the sitting-room. Richard had been right. She had held on to her pride. But at what cost?

'Darling', he had called her. But it couldn't have meant anything. How could it, when he himself had told her that he had never loved her, never felt anything for her other than hatred and contempt? She buried her head in the cushions of the sofa, giving way to the storm of misery engulfing her.

Now, at last, she could admit the truth. She loved him, and she would continue to love him, no matter what he had done to her.

CHAPTER TEN

THE first intimation Susannah had that she wasn't alone was the sudden touch of cherishing male hands taking hold of her and turning her round.

Hazard was kneeling on the floor at her side, his face taut with despair and pain.

'Oh, my darling, please don't! I can't bear to see you like this.' His hands cupped her face, his lips caressing her skin. She wanted to push him away, but she felt too weak.

Instead she protested huskily, 'Stop it... Stop it, Hazard. I don't need your pity.'

She felt him tense. 'We must talk.'

'There's nothing to talk about.' She would have given anything for him not to have seen her like this. 'You've already said it all—remember?'

She wasn't able to keep the bitterness from her voice and, to her shock, Hazard bowed his head, his voice tormented as he protested rawly, 'Please don't. You can't know how I've regretted...'

'I *know* you're sorry, Hazard. Richard's already told me that,' she interrupted him bleakly. 'I don't know why you've come here—or for what. If it's absolution, then you've got it. From what Richard's told me about your background, I can understand why you felt the need to protect their marriage.'

'No... no, that isn't why I came, Susannah. Look at me...' His hands tilted her face so that she was forced to look into his eyes. They were dark with emotion, agonised with pain, containing a despair she recognised from her own reflection. Her heartbeat slowed and then jerked frantically. 'I love you.'

She heard the words, but couldn't respond to them.

'I had to tell you that.'

'You said I meant nothing to you,' she whispered miserably.

'I lied...'

She searched his face for some sign that his words were cruel lies, designed to torment her, but all she could see was his pain and humility. But even then she couldn't believe it.

'You can't love me,' she told him with painful honesty. 'I've been involved with a married man. I...'

His fingers trembled oddly against her lips as he silenced her. 'No... Don't. Please, don't.'

'But it's true,' she protested huskily. 'David...'

'I know all about that.' His voice was harsh. 'I went to see your aunt after...'

Susannah waited, expecting to hear him say after he had learned the truth. Instead, to her shock, he said, 'After you didn't come back to the office. We had a long talk. I confessed to her how badly I'd treated you, and she told me all about what happened with David.'

'*Aunt Emily* did? But she knows nothing...'

His wry grimace silenced her.

'I think you'll find she knows far more about you than you realise. She told me how concerned she'd been when she had heard gossip that you were involved with David, and how upset she'd been when you had told her you were leaving home. She guessed why, and was proud of you for your decision.' He looked away from her for a moment, his face bleak. 'I went to see him. I couldn't find you anywhere and I thought...'

'That I'd gone to *David*?'

'I was desperate,' he told her simply. 'I had to find you. Instead, I saw his wife. She told me everything that had happened. That you and her husband had never actually been lovers, and that you hadn't even realised he was married, at first.'

Susannah remembered telling Louise those facts, but she had never dreamed that they would be repeated to Hazard.

'Even if you and David *had* been lovers, it wouldn't alter how I feel about you,' Hazard told her emotionally. 'It couldn't. I've had to do a lot of thinking these last few weeks, Susannah. I've had to accept that love is far too strong an emotion to be cast aside lightly.'

'You can't love me.'

She was trembling wildly beneath the fingers that touched her skin with such tender concern.

'You mean, you don't *want* me to love you? I can't blame you for that,' he said sombrely. 'Believe me, I didn't come up here to burden you with my emotions.'

'Then why *did* you come?'

'Because I had to,' he answered honestly. 'I couldn't eat, I couldn't sleep, I couldn't work...'

'Richard told me you were in New York,' she said inconsequentially, not really knowing what to say, what to believe.

'I was. My mother had another heart attack.'

A spasm of pain crossed his face, and instinctively she reached out to touch him. An electrifying sensation shot through her as her fingertips came into contact with the hard maleness of his skin. A dark shadow was already developing where he shaved, tiny bristles prickling against her flesh.

'This time it was fatal. I know that, for her, death is a merciful release from a life that became unendurable the moment my father walked out on us. All my life, I've fought against that knowledge, fought against admitting that I carry within me the genes of a human being so vulnerable to love. All my life, for as long as I can remember, I've sworn that nothing like that would ever happen to me, that I'd never give my happiness into someone else's keeping.'

This was the communication between them that she had wanted; this was the lowering of the barrier she had sensed within him, but all she could feel was a hollow numbness, an inability to believe that any of it was real.

'I should go.' He released her and stood up. 'I promised Emma I wouldn't overstrain you.'

'Emma knows you're here?'

'Yes,' he told her quietly, holding her shocked gaze. 'I rang her the other morning when I got back from the States. She told me to ring back.'

Of course! The phone call that preceded her trip to the village.

'I managed to persuade her to allow me to come up to see you. She said it would be best if I saw you alone...'

'Oh, Emma!'

'Don't blame her. She told me you had said you didn't want to see me.'

But she had still gone and left her here alone, not warning her what to expect, Susannah reflected numbly.

He was walking towards the door and out of her life. He turned the handle and breathlessly she called out, 'Hazard! That night, when you came to my flat, when you accused me of having an affair with Richard and you said that you had never wanted me...'

He turned slowly to face her, his face haggard.

'I'd just flown in from New York. They'd told me that this time my mother really was dying. All the way back, during the flight, I kept remembering how often she had tried to die. I went straight from the airport to your flat. I couldn't think of anything other than how much I needed to be with you... I wanted to lose myself, my past, in the warm sweetness of you... I couldn't believe it when I saw you in Richard's car. It was as though all my nightmares had suddenly come true.

'I lied to you that night, Susannah. I hit out at you in my torment and said and did things I know can never be forgotten, not by you and certainly not by me. After I left you, I went back to my flat, already regretting every word I'd said and cursing myself for a fool. I told myself I should have stayed and fought for you, made you love me instead of Richard. I went round to see you the next day, but your flat was empty, and you weren't at work. I told myself you must be with Richard, so I went home and demolished the best part of a full bottle of whisky.'

He grimaced distastefully. 'That, on top of the jet lag I was already suffering, knocked me out completely, and that was how Caroline found me.'

'And then you started to look for me; after you knew the truth.' She spoke almost absently.

'Yes, but I would have looked for you anyway. The way I feel about you has nothing to do with whether or not any of your past lovers have been married. There's no way I can prove that to you, though, Susannah, just as there's no way I can ask you to take me on trust. You gave me your trust and I abused it, and that's something I'll have to live with for the rest of my life.'

He opened the door, and she felt as though a vice tightened painfully inside her. She could let him go, and remain secure within the citadel of her pride, or she could open herself once more to pain and hurt by risking believing in him. The choice was hers.

He had reached the back door before she was able to make it.

'Hazard.'

The moment she spoke his name he stopped, waiting, watching her with such a look of agonised tension in his eyes that she could have wept for him as well as herself.

'Please stay.'

Two words, and yet they meant so much. He came back to her, trembling as he caught hold of her.

'If this is just a dream, I pray I never wake up from it,' he said fervently, as his hands shaped the narrowness of her back, their touch warm and comforting. 'I don't deserve this. I promise, somehow I'll try to find a way of making it all up to you. I won't ask you to love me, Susannah, not yet. But . . .'

She shook her head, interrupting him. 'If I didn't love you, I wouldn't be doing this,' she told him quietly. 'Oh, I've tried to deny it, tried to fight against what I feel for you, but I can't.'

'Will you hate me if I tell you that I'm glad?' he asked thickly, bending his head towards her.

She tensed instinctively, avoiding his kiss, pain shadowing her eyes as she slipped out of his arms. 'You must be hungry. It's a long drive up here; I'll make you something to eat.'

Could this really be her, chattering nervously, dreading the thought of him touching her? What was wrong with her? She loved him, and yet the moment he came close to her she became confused and fearful. Was the trust she had once felt completely gone?

Hazard let her go without a word, but she saw the pain she felt mirrored in his eyes.

She loved him and he was here with her, but something was stopping her from reaching out to him.

Quietly, he agreed that he *would* like something to eat, helping her with the meal and then with the clearing up afterwards.

Early in the evening, Emma rang, apologising for the trick she had played. They both spoke to her but, after the telephone call had finished, a tense silence engulfed the sitting-room.

Despite the warmth, Susannah shivered, hugging her arms around herself. Since her rebuff in the afternoon, Hazard had made no attempt to touch her. Instead, he had talked to her, describing to her his childhood, laying bare for her to see the miseries it had contained. Slowly, he encouraged her to share *her* childhood memories with him, and as she did so she had a new image of her aunt, as a lonely and rather tragic woman who had wanted to do all she could for the child in her care, but who had no way of showing her love for her. Her aunt *did* love her, Susannah recognised now. It was just that she had never been able to show it. Her sternness, her determination that Susannah would grow up in what she considered to be the right way—these had been her ways of showing that love.

'I want us to be married,' Hazard told her abruptly. 'We belong together, you and I, Susannah.'

She couldn't deny his words. She didn't *want* to, she admitted.

A quiver of sensation pulsed through her, a tight coiling sweetness that she instantly controlled.

As she bent towards the fire they had lit earlier in the evening, her hair slid forward. Hazard reached out to tuck it behind her ear, and instantly she froze. His hand dropped away, his face gaunt with remorse.

'What is it Susannah? Why are you so repelled by my touch?'

'Not repelled.' Her voice shook, and colour surged up under her pale face. 'I can't explain it, Hazard.' She turned to look at him, her eyes dark with bewilderment. 'I know I love you, but somewhere deep inside I'm frightened...'

She actually shivered as she spoke, as though that cold finger of fear was spreading within her.

'Of me?'

She shook her head. 'Of what I felt when you left me...when you said you didn't love me.'

He groaned, the tautness of his face revealed to her in the firelight, its bone structure stark and sharply drawn. Like her, he had lost weight. She wanted so badly to reach out and touch him, but something prevented her.

'I've hurt you so much. What can I say? What can I do?'

Susannah shook her head, her voice low and uneven. 'I don't know.'

Hazard reached out to her, as though to comfort her, and then withdrew.

'You need time,' he told her gently. 'I can't blame you for not trusting me. In your shoes . . . Would you like me to leave? To find somewhere to stay in the village tonight?'

His offer touched her. She had been so afraid that he would rush her; that he would try to make love to her. Part of her almost wanted to do that, she recognised, but another part knew that she wasn't ready or able to give him that sort of commitment at the moment.

But neither did she want him to leave.

'Please stay,' she whispered. 'I can make up the bed in the room you had before.'

'If that's what you want.'

It was late when they finally went to bed. The evening had passed quickly as they talked, its peacefulness broken only by the odd tense moment when Hazard came close to forgetting how she felt and instinctively reached out to touch her, only to withdraw as he remembered.

Her eyelids had been feeling heavy for half an hour or so, but she had fought to stay awake.

'You're tired. It's time you went to bed,' Hazard told her roughly, adding with a grim whiteness around his mouth, 'You needn't be afraid I'm going to force myself on you, Susannah. It's you, the person, I want, not just a body to share my bed.'

Beneath the grimness, she caught the note of pain and ached to reassure him that he was wrong and that she didn't fear him in the way he thought. What she really feared was herself and the intensity of her reaction to him, she admitted. It left her feeling vulnerable and afraid. And now that fear was already coming between them.

Once in bed, she lay there, unable to sleep. The house was still, and she could hear the creak of the bed as Hazard, like herself, moved restlessly within it. How could she conquer her fear? She shivered, seeing with feminine wisdom how easily it could destroy their relationship. Trust was such a tender plant.

It was her inexperience that lay at the root of her fear, she recognised wisely. The realisation of the strength of her own sexuality, followed so quickly by Hazard's rejection of her, had created a deep-rooted dread of the abandonment that desire aroused within her. And there was only one way such a fear could be overcome, she acknowledged, trembling within the secure warmth of her bed.

Hazard's room was in darkness, but he saw her walk in and sat up in bed.

'Susannah.' She saw the way his muscles clenched as he said her name in a harsh, unfamiliar voice. 'For God's sake, don't look at me like that!'

For a moment, she was hurt, and then she realised that she was arousing him. Her pulse rate doubled, her heart thudding frantically. She touched her tongue to her dry lips, a feverish, frantic heat spreading through her body. She shuddered, and Hazard got out of bed, cursing as he saw her widening gaze take in his nudity.

'Susannah, what is it? Are you ill?'

For a moment, she stared at him blankly; she felt both hot and cold, weak and strong, terrified and brave.

'I want you to make love to me.'

He froze where he stood, searching her face in the shadows of the moonlight.

When he spoke, his voice was rough and strained.

'Susannah, think about this. I don't want to do anything to hurt you. Once I take you in my arms . . . Once I touch you . . .' He groaned, and his body shook, as though possessed by a fever. 'I'm only a man, only human, and I've been aching for the feel of your skin against my own for what feels like a lifetime.'

He was giving her the opportunity to withdraw, and in that moment Susannah felt a tremendous surge of love flood her body. The fear was still there, but it was receding. She took a step towards him, and then another. His arms opened and she half ran and half stumbled into them. They closed around her, and she felt the fierce tremble of his flesh.

Like her, he too was vulnerable.

Before he picked her up and carried her back to the bed, he kissed her, feathering his lips gently against hers, until he felt her response, and then his kiss hardened, deepened, betraying his need of her. His mouth released hers, his fingers tracing the moistly swollen outline of her lips.

'Oh, God, you don't know what you do to me, darling. You make me want you so much.'

She trembled slightly as she felt the force of his passion in the aroused heat of his body.

'Don't be afraid of me, Susannah. I know I hurt you, but try to understand, it was a hurt born of jealousy and despair. I misjudged you. I can never forgive myself for that.'

She touched her fingers to his lips to silence him. 'It's over, Hazard. We both made mistakes. But there's something I still have to tell you.'

She felt him tense against her body and she shivered in response. What if he rejected her now? What if he found the fact of her inexperience unacceptable? She had a momentary cowardly impulse not to tell him, but she had been brought up in total honesty and she knew that she couldn't. Surely, in her inexperience, she would betray the truth anyway, and then he would know that she had deceived him. Their new relationship must not begin under the shadow of any more deceit.

'What is it?'

His voice was harsh, forbiddingly so.

'Hazard, I... You know that I never had a physical relationship with David, but ... there hasn't been that kind of relationship in my life *at all*.'

For a moment, Hazard was so still that she daren't look at him. What a fool he must think her, and she didn't blame him. Pain clogged her throat, her chest a tight mass of constricted muscle that made it almost impossible for her to breathe.

'I'm sorry,' she whispered huskily, bending her head so that he couldn't see the pain in her eyes.

'*You're* sorry! Oh, God, Susannah, I'm the one who should be saying that. When I think what I've said to you...what I've done. I'll find a way to make it up to you, I promise you. No wonder you backed off from me! I must have half terrified you out of your life,' he said roughly. 'It needn't be like that, my darling, I promise you. I was jealous and angry, driven almost out of my mind by the way I felt about you...'

'It isn't you I'm frightened of,' Susannah interrupted him, shocked by the bitter self-hatred in his voice. 'It's me.'

He tensed and she looked at him, seeing the bleakness in his eyes. She took a deep breath to steady herself.

'I wanted you so much, Hazard. It frightened me——'

The rest of what she had been going to say was smothered beneath the fierce pressure of his mouth, quickly gentled, as though he was fighting to get himself under control.

As he picked her up and carried her over to the bed, he said quickly, 'I want to make love to you, Susannah, but you have to want it as well. For now, just let me hold you in my arms, otherwise I'm not going to be able to believe that you're real.'

She didn't want just to be held in his arms, Susannah acknowledged on a shocked spurt of surprise. She wanted to feel his hands on her skin, his mouth...his warmth and heat...the strength of him around and within her.

As he lay down beside her, she reached out to him, sliding awkwardly out of her robe, pressing her body eagerly against his. She felt him shudder and then his hands were on her skin, the heat of his nearness searing her. He was breathing harshly, the ragged sound filling the silence.

A fierce surge of desire arched her wantonly against him, the damp heat of his skin, moving rhythmically against her own, a sensual excitement that made her gasp and shiver, her fear forgotten as she clung eagerly to him.

Hazard whispered her name, his throat arched with tension. Her tongue stroked its rigid lines, tasting the musky flavour of his sweat. He groaned, shuddering at her touch, his voice hoarse and disjointed as he moaned his need.

'Oh God, Susannah, I want you so much. Give yourself to me, my darling. Trust me...'

And, unbelievably, she did. Her fear was gone, her body reacting joyously to his physical and vocal urging.

She felt the first thrust of his penetration and her flesh welcomed it. The heat and strength of him inside made her cry out with pleasure, but instantly Hazard tensed, his eyes dark with remorse as they focused on hers. He started to withdraw from her, but she clung to him, deliberately moving arousingly against him. With an anguished protest, he surrendered to the need within him. His body filled hers. Waves of pleasure gathered her up, carrying her onwards to an impossible crest.

They reached it together, their bodies sharing the exquisite release. Their heartbeats and breathing hurried, Hazard crying out her name in a long low sound of ecstasy, before collapsing against her.

Tenderly, she held him, marvelling that she could ever have been afraid of this joyous closeness, this oneness.

When he had his breathing back under control, Hazard took her in his arms and said huskily, 'Tonight was a first for me, too. Never has there been a time when I've felt the way you made me feel just now. Before, sex was just an appetite that I satisfied within the parameters of my relationships. I've never gone in for casual sex. It's never appealed, but neither have I ever felt for anyone else what I feel for you.'

'And that made a difference?' Susannah asked softly, shivering slightly as she remembered the intensity of the way he had made love to her.

'All the difference in the world,' he told her huskily, touching his tongue to her parted lips. 'We'll have to marry almost straight away, so now is the time to voice your objections.'

'I've no objections,' Susannah told him. Her doubts and fears had gone, disappeared like a mirage faced with reality. 'But why straight away?'

Hazard grimaced slightly. 'I wasn't exactly controlled when I made love to you, and when I came up here the consequences of any lovemaking were the last thing on my mind.' His hand covered her stomach. 'You could have conceived my child.'

'If I have, will you mind?'

'Not unless you do.'

She smiled dreamily at him. 'I wonder if Emma would agree to be godmother.'

'Why don't we ask her?' Hazard suggested softly. 'But not right now . . . right now, I have other things on my mind.'

He bent his head and started to kiss her again.

IN A WORLD OF DECEIT
AND FORBIDDEN DESIRE
TRUTH IS A
DOUBLE-EDGED
SWORD

TELL
ME
NO
LIES

ELIZABETH
LOWELL

Conscience, scandal and desire.

A dynamic story of a woman whose integrity, both personal and professional, is compromised by the intrigue that surrounds her.

Against a background of corrupt Chinese government officials, the CIA and a high powered international art scandal, Lindsay Danner becomes the perfect pawn in a deadly game. Only ex-CIA hit man Catlin can ensure she succeeds... and lives.

Together they find a love which will unite them and overcome the impossible odds they face.

Available May. Price £3.50

W●RLDWIDE

Available from Boots, Martins, John Menzies, W.H. Smith, Woolworths and other paperback stockists.

YOU'RE INVITED TO ACCEPT **FOUR ROMANCES** AND A TOTE BAG **FREE!**

Acceptance card

| NO STAMP NEEDED | Post to: Reader Service, FREEPOST, P.O. Box 236, Croydon, Surrey. CR9 9EL |

Please note readers in Southern Africa write to:
Independant Book Services P.T.Y., Postbag X3010, Randburg 2125, S. Africa

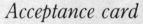

YES! Please send me 4 free Mills & Boon Romances and my free tote bag – and reserve a Reader Service Subscription for me. If I decide to subscribe I shall receive 6 new Romances every month as soon as they come off the presses for £7.20 together with a FREE monthly newsletter including information on top authors and special offers, exclusively for Reader Service subscribers. There are no postage and packing charges, and I understand I may cancel or suspend my subscription at any time. If I decide not to subscribe I shall write to you within 10 days. Even if I decide not to subscribe the 4 free novels and the tote bag are mine to keep forever. I am over 18 years of age   EP20R

NAME _____

                                        (CAPITALS PLEASE)

ADDRESS _____

_____

_____ POSTCODE _____

Mills & Boon Ltd. reserve the right to exercise discretion in
granting membership. You may be mailed with other offers as a
result of this application. Offer expires June 30th 1988 and is
limited to one per household.
Offer applies in UK and Eire only. Overseas send for details.

They were survivors, both of them... But could they overcome the scars of war?

In post World War One Paris there is a new era, full of hope and determination to build a brilliant future.

Alix Morell is one of the new young women, whose strong will and new-found independence helps her face the challenges ahead.

Jake Sherwood is a Canadian pilot who had fought his way to the top – but whose dreams are shattered in one last cruel moment of war.

Can Alix release Jake from his self-made prison?

Their compelling love story is poignantly portrayed in Ann Hulme's latest bestselling novel.

Published June 1988   **Price £2.95**

W●RLDWIDE

Available from Boots, Martins, John Menzies, W H Smith, Woolworths and other paperback stockists

AND THEN HE KISSED HER...

This is the title of our new venture — an audio tape designed to help you become a successful Mills & Boon author!

In the past, those of you who asked us for advice on how to write for Mills & Boon have been supplied with brief printed guidelines. Our new tape expands on these and, by carefully chosen examples, shows you how to make your story come alive. And we think you'll enjoy listening to it.

You can still get the printed guidelines by writing to our Editorial Department. But, if you would like to have the tape, please send a cheque or postal order for £4.95 (which includes VAT and postage) to:

VAT REG. No. 232 4334 96

- -

AND THEN HE KISSED HER...
To: Mills & Boon Reader Service, FREEPOST, P.O. Box 236, Croydon, Surrey CR9 9EL.

Please send me _____ copies of the audio tape. I enclose a cheque/postal order*, crossed and made payable to Mills & Boon Reader Service, for the sum of £_____. *Please delete whichever is not applicable.

Signature _____

Name (BLOCK LETTERS) _____

Address _____

_____ Post Code _____
YOU MAY BE MAILED WITH OTHER OFFERS AS A RESULT OF THIS APPLICATION   ED1